***The sound of the rain grew louder overhead, and there was a loud crack of thunder.***

"Male rain," Will said, watching the trees bend under the onslaught of the rising storm.

"Rain has a gender?"

"Where I come from it does."

"What's a female rain like?"

"Steady. Gentle. Soft."

After a moment Arley stepped closer.

"I know you're tough – Airborne and all that – and I don't want you to panic because this is not because I think you need it," she said. "This is because I need it – so *I'll* feel better."

With that, she slid her arms around him, resting her head against his shoulder.

He intended to end the embrace, to step away while he still could, but she lifted her head and looked at him. She was so close, her body soft and warm against his. He tried to smile and didn't quite make it. Instead, he slowly lowered his mouth to lightly touch hers.

# Available in June 2008
# from Mills & Boon®
# Special Edition

# Medicine Man
# CHERYL REAVIS

MILLS & BOON®
*Pure reading pleasure*

*First published in Great Britain 2008
by Harlequin Mills & Boon Limited,
Eton House, 18-24 Paradise Road, Richmond, Surrey TW9 1SR*

© Cheryl Reavis 2007

*ISBN: 978 0 263 86053 5*

23-0608

*Harlequin Mills & Boon policy is to use papers that are natural, renewable and recyclable products and made from wood grown in sustainable forests. The logging and manufacturing processes conform to the legal environmental regulations of the country of origin.*

*Printed and bound in Spain
by Litografía Rosés S.A., Barcelona*

For all the readers who have written to ask me
what happened to Will Baron.
This is for you, with my sincere thanks for
your kind comments and support.

Special thanks, too, to Vanessa's sergeant
for answering my many questions.
Any mistakes are mine, not his.

## CHERYL REAVIS

award-winning short story author and romance
novelist who also writes under the name of Cinda
Richards, describes herself as a late bloomer
who played in her first piano recital at the tender
age of thirty. "We had to line up by height – I
was the third smallest kid," she says. "After that,
there was no stopping me. I immediately gave
myself permission to attempt my other heart's
desire – to write." Her Special Edition novel *A
Crime of the Heart* reached millions of readers
via *Good Housekeeping* magazine. Both *A Crime
of the Heart* and *Patrick Gallagher's Widow* won
the Romance Writers of America's coveted
RITA® Award for Best Contemporary Series
Romance the year they were published. *One
of Our Own* received the Career Achievement
Award for Best Innovative Series Romance from
*Romantic Times BOOKreviews*. A former public
health nurse, Cheryl makes her home in North
Carolina with her husband.

Dear Reader,

What a capricious thing a writer's muse can be. More than once I've thought a character's story had ended only to discover that that wasn't the case at all. They're still there somehow, but out of sight, waiting for just the right opportunity to step into the limelight again.

I first encountered Will Baron when he was three years old, and what a great writing pleasure it was to create a better life for this abandoned little boy. Will was happy. End of story. Or so I thought.

Then, here he came again when he was a teenager, both helping and needing help, filling an important supportive role in other stories I wanted to tell and yet still yearning for things he would have been hard pressed to name.

And now, here he is one more time – with his own story at last. *Medicine Man* is Will Baron's journey to finally find the place where he truly belongs and to win the heart of the woman he is struggling so hard not to love.

I hope you'll enjoy reading it, and I hope you'll visit me at my website: www.members. authorsguild.net/cherylreavis/

Best always,

*Cheryl Reavis*

## Chapter One

*I never should have come.*

Arley Meehan stood in the middle of her sister Kate's boisterous wedding reception, trying not to look as miserable as she felt. The pub was packed with military personnel, the Airborne contingent from Fort Bragg, courtesy of Kate's new husband—*his* side of the family, as it were. She was happy for Kate, for them both—of *course* she was—and she had wanted this opportunity to get out and have a good time for a change. But weddings were no place for the newly-divorced, no matter how bad the marriage had been, and Arley wished now that she had stayed home with her little boy for an evening of fast food and popcorn, a rented movie and lots of giggling.

The Celtic/bluegrass band her uncle Patrick had hired for the occasion suddenly straddled both genres and began to play a wooden-whistle-and-banjo-spiked rendition of "Sally Goodin," much to the delight of the guests. A few of the more adventurous couples began to dance, whether they actually knew how to or not, making Arley's immediate vicinity a dangerous place to be. She moved out of the way, dodging a number of low dips and high kicks in the process, and she recognized a soldier standing alone on the other side of the pub. She knew his name—Specialist Will Baron. He was a medic who worked with Kate at the post hospital and, at the moment, was looking every bit as alone as she felt. Arley had met him once, in passing, last summer, before she and her sisters had even noticed that Kate had been well on her way to marrying a seriously injured paratrooper.

Arley swiftly headed in his direction. She had been given a token assignment for the night—something her oldest sister, Grace, had devised to keep Arley the Handful out of trouble. She was supposed to circulate among the guests and make sure everyone was having a good time, which had seemed totally unnecessary until now. Clearly, Will Baron was the place to start.

"So how homesick are you?" she asked when she reached him.

He looked around, his quick double take suggesting he remembered who she was.

"Arley Meehan," she said anyway. "Welcome to the Kate Meehan-Cal Doyle wedding festivities. Are you having a good time, Specialist Baron?"

"Yes," he said politely.

She gave him an arch look. "Not true, I think."

He almost smiled. "Actually, I…forgot how much I missed it…these family things."

*So did I,* she thought. She had missed her sisters terribly, despite deliberately isolating herself from them for a long time. The humiliation of having been betrayed by the man she'd loved, of having made yet another bad choice by marrying him in the first place, had been too much for her. She'd needed to have time to recover and regroup, and to get over the fact that her sisters had been so right and she had been so glaringly wrong. Tonight was really her first big venture back into the fold.

"How's Scottie?" Will asked, and she smiled.

She'd forgotten that her son had been with her when she and Will Baron had run into each other last summer. "You remembered his name," she said in surprise.

"It's something I do—remember things. Is he still collecting rocks?"

"Still," she said. "At the moment, though, he wants to go on the honeymoon."

"Well, that ought to be…interesting."

"Especially since he's learned to make armpit noises."

He grinned—something Arley decided he should definitely do more often.

"Good for him," he said. "Is he here tonight?"

"No, he and the rest of the cousins are having their own wild party—pizza and video games and wedding cake with the great-aunts. I think he'd rather be elsewhere. Tonight's our regular fast food and movie rental night. So where are you from?"

There was a lull in the music, leaving a strange gap in the din around them.

"Arizona. Window Rock. The Navajo Reservation."

"So you're…Navajo?"

"Half," he said. "My birth mother is one of The People."

"Your birth mother?" she asked, but he didn't respond to her clear invitation to elaborate.

"You were brought up with…'The People,' I take it," she said, deciding to respect his reticence. She had plenty of things she didn't want to talk about, either.

"With. By. For," he said.

"And your father—what was he?" she asked, without considering whether it was polite to do so. She wanted to know, and she had earned her "Arley the Handful" title as much from being curious as from being reckless.

The band started up again, as lively as ever.

"A Tar Heel," he said over the racket. "Full-blooded."

She smiled, appreciating his reference to his father having been born in North Carolina.

"Is he from around here?"

"Not exactly," he said.

"What does that mean?"

"He…died when I was three. I don't know much about him, actually."

"Oh. I'm sorry. Well, you can always kill two birds with one stone," she said, and he gave her a puzzled look.

The noise escalated, and she leaned closer to explain.

"If I'd joined the army to see the world…" she began, trying to make herself heard over the drumbeats.

"I think that's the navy," he interrupted.

"Whatever. If I'd joined the army to see the world and I'd ended up in the state where my long lost father had lived, I'd probably try to check it out. Especially if I didn't know much about him. Two birds. See?"

He didn't say whether he did or didn't. The music suddenly softened, enough so she didn't need to yell anymore.

"Was it hard to get sent to Fort Bragg?" she asked, disregarding his lack of enthusiasm for her opinion that he might find a personal advantage to being posted here.

"Well, it took a certain amount of jumping out of high- and low-flying aircraft."

"I'll bet—"

"Who's this?" a man's voice said behind her, and Arley froze. She had no doubt that the question was meant for her.

"Will Baron—coworker of the bride," Will said easily, extending his hand to her ex-husband, someone who was *not* supposed to be here.

"Scott McGowan," Scott said pointedly. "So just how do you know *him?*" he asked Arley, ignoring Will's outstretched hand.

Arley forced herself to look at him—and didn't answer. She knew he'd take offense at whatever comment she made, and she wasn't about to let him cause a scene in the middle of Kate's reception. She glanced past him at the guests. She couldn't see any of her sisters.

"I asked you a question, Arley," Scott said, his voice deceptively calm. She didn't miss the menace behind the remark, the subtle threat of consequences, and, neither, she thought, did Will Baron.

"So you did, Scott," she said agreeably. She smiled and didn't continue. He didn't appreciate it.

"Let's go outside—*now*," he said. He reached to take her arm, and she jerked back. Will moved, putting himself between her and Scott, close enough to keep Scott at bay and still leave room for him to back down— if he had enough sense.

"Do you want to go with him?" Will asked her.

"No," Arley said, hating that she couldn't keep her voice steady.

"That's good enough for me," Will said. "For them, too," he added, nodding toward the nearby group of paratroopers, who were already on the alert and looking in their direction.

Will and Scott stared at each other.

"Excuse me," Arley said abruptly. "It was interesting talking to you, Specialist," she said to Will. Then she did what she did best—walked off and left the mess she had created.

"Arley! What do you want from me?" Scott called after her, as if she were the unreasonable one.

*Nothing,* she thought. And that in itself was a revelation. She didn't want, didn't need, anything from him anymore.

She kept walking, dodging the dancers, knowing Scott was likely following her. He didn't give up easily. The real question was, what did *he* want?

She could see Uncle Patrick working hard behind the crowded bar, and she headed in that direction.

"Ah! Reinforcements!" he said when he saw her. "Find yourself an apron, darlin'. I need another pair of hands."

Arley slipped behind the bar. Her knees were shaking as she found an apron and managed to wrap it around herself, taking her place next to her uncle, rushing to fill mug after mug with beer.

"Steady now," Uncle Patrick said quietly. "Scottie is safe with the aunts and he-who-shall-not-be-named has taken himself out the door."

When she finally got the nerve to look up, she didn't see Scott anywhere. She didn't see Will Baron, either.

She bowed her head again and filled another mug. So much for getting out and having a good time.

"What was *that* all about?"

Will glanced at Specialist Bernie Copus and considered his options. He could answer the question now and get it over with, or he could answer it any one of the thousands of times Copus would ask for the rest of their natural lives.

"I thought you were going to clean that young man's clock for him," Copus said. He grinned, showing the gap between his front teeth, a feature women found irresistible.

Or so he said.

"I don't know what it was about," Will said, hoping the truth would bring an end to the interrogation. All he had understood of the situation was that Arley Meehan had been afraid.

"Listen to your old Uncle Bernie, now. I have to admit the former Mrs. McGowan is a good-looking woman—a *good*-looking woman. But, you're not wanting to go *there,* son, believe me. You're not wanting to get between the McGowan heir and something he prizes. No sirree."

"Copus, I'm not—"

"No, now, I am serious, William. I know how this thing works."

"And how is that?"

"*You* are in the military. *He* is in the money. His family owns the whole damn world. What do you own?"

"Not much," Will said.

"Well, there you go. Need I say more?"

"I hope not."

Copus grinned, showing his gap again. "I'm just trying to help you out, son."

"Yeah, and how much is that going to cost me?" Will asked, because Specialist Copus was nothing if not mercenary.

"Not one cent—this time. I can see how tempting that little flower is, but I'm telling you, this thing has got trouble written all over it. I am a man of vast experience and I know."

"Copus, I told you. It's not—" Will stopped. "I don't even know her."

"Okay, okay. You just think of me as that television robot—the one that looks like an old-time wringer washing machine—and I'm going, 'Danger, Will Baron!'"

Copus waved his arms for emphasis, knocking somebody's beer to the floor in the process. Will grinned and walked away, leaving Copus to do what he did so well, apologize profusely in the hopes of not getting pitched across the premises.

The music stopped abruptly as the band made room on the small stage for the bride and groom to say farewell and get on with married life. Will joined in the toasts, laughing at the heavy-handed newlywed commentaries served up by a number of the paratrooper guests. He was determined to enjoy the rest of the evening. Even without Copus's dubious advice, Will knew better than to get involved in whatever was going on between the bride's sister and her ex-husband. He deliberately stood so he could see Arley out of the corner of his eye, however. She stayed behind the bar, participating in one toast after another, just as he did, laughing in all the right places and, as far as he could tell, completely unaffected by the incident earlier.

Except that he didn't think that was the case.

The bride and groom were leaving—or trying to. Clearly, it was the custom for everyone at the postnuptial party to escort them to their car. The band members struck up another song, playing as they walked, a reprise of something they'd done earlier.

Will stood back to let them pass, losing track of Arley in the surge of people heading toward the door.

He was one of the last to reach the outside, and he had to force himself into the mugginess of the summer night. He had grown up in the desert and he was used to hot temperatures, but he would never adjust to the oppressive heat and humidity so rampant in this part of the country. He always felt as if he were walking into a living being.

The band played as enthusiastically as ever, but outside the music dissipated into the night air.

"So how homesick are you?" someone said.

Arley stood on the sidewalk near the door.

"Not very," he said this time. He realized she was starting their conversation over, rewinding it to the point *before* her ex-husband arrived.

"Really," he added, and she smiled.

"Maybe you ought to tell your face that."

"Aren't you going to go say goodbye to Kate?" he said to divert the conversation to a safer topic.

"I did earlier. Besides, I might catch the bouquet."

"Wouldn't want to do that, I guess."

"No way. So I thought I'd annoy you instead."

"Any…particular reason?"

"Yes," she said without hesitation. "You're so *serene.* Even when you're not having a good time."

He laughed softly, because, at this moment, she couldn't have been more wrong.

"Is that a Navajo thing?"

"What?"

"Serenity," she said pointedly. "Pay attention, Baron."

"It's kind of hard to do both—be serene *and* pay attention," he said, smiling still.

"Just answer the question."

"Which one?"

"The serenity one."

"Yes. It's a Navajo thing."

"Must be hard to do—in the military, I mean."

"Sometimes."

"Now answer the other question. How homesick are you?"

He drew a quiet breath, aware of the night sounds around them, the kind that didn't mean home to him. "Well, all the pine trees help—except they're too tall and the wrong variety."

"That's what I thought. Did you leave a girl behind? In Window Rock?"

"Ah…no," he said.

"A lot of family, though."

"A lot, yes."

"How many brothers and sisters?"

"One half brother. One half sister."

"That's not a lot."

"Well, my half sister—Meggie—has children—hers and the rest of the world's. Stray people are Meggie's thing. And there's my stepfather—Lucas Singer—he's also my uncle by marriage, because he married my father's sister, Sloan, who got joint custody with the tribe so she could raise me. Lucas has a sister—she's a lawyer, the kick-butt kind. She's got children, plus there's the daughter my stepfather-uncle by marriage didn't know he had and her husband, Ben. Ben's a tribal policeman. So is my stepfather-uncle and his sister the lawyer's husband."

"Go on," she said, when he stopped his deliberately convoluted recital to see if her eyes had glazed over. Incredibly, she was listening.

"And then there are the non-blood-related people who have a permanent invitation to attend any and all Baron-Singer social gatherings—the ones who are just passing by and happen to smell dinner cooking, and the ones in and out of jail. Basically, it's the Navajo reservation version of Mayberry."

She laughed softly. It pleased him to make her laugh.

"What about your birth mother? Does she come?"

"No. She doesn't. Meggie would invite her, though, if she got the chance. She's like that."

"What about your half brother?"

"Patrick. He's…" Will stopped. There were no precise adjectives for Patrick. He was and always had been a walking contradiction.

"So when was the last time you were home?" Arley asked.

"Christmas. Are we…going someplace with this?" he asked.

"I like to know things," she said. "Especially when it comes from somebody who doesn't like to tell them."

"Well, that would be me," he said. "Usually."

"And this usual…reticence—is that a Navajo thing or a Tar Heel thing?"

"Can't be a Tar Heel thing," he said, making her smile again.

"Don't go by me. Some Tar Heels are reticent," she assured him. "Do you like being in the army?"

"It's what I need," he said cryptically. He had never really articulated to anyone why he'd enlisted—there were a lot of reasons, including a very persuasive army recruiter with a quota to meet. But the most important ones had to do with Will's obligation to and affection for the people who had rescued him after his father was killed and had given him a good life.

Two women stood watching them from the edge of the crowd surrounding the Meehan-Doyle getaway car. One was strong-looking and tall and unyielding, like a tree that would break rather than bend. The other seemed tentative and anxious, as if she had more concerns than she could handle. Both of them looked just enough like Arley and Kate for him to hazard a guess.

"I think I see two of your relatives," he said when the women's intense interest began to exceed his comfort level.

"My sisters," Arley said. "Gwen and Grace, the micromanagers. Kate is usually their target. Lucky me, I get to be their surrogate concern for the next two weeks."

"Kate's only going to be gone three days."

"It's going to seem like two weeks," Arley assured him.

"It's…good to have relatives who care."

"You think so?"

"Where I grew up, it is. The worst thing you can do is behave as if you didn't have anyone who cared enough about you to teach you right from wrong."

"Now, that's a Tar Heel thing. It's called 'not being raised.' Don't ever act like you haven't been raised, Baron. People would talk. It would reflect badly on your father's family forever, and, believe me, you don't want that."

Arley paused. "Will, thank you," she said suddenly.

"For…?"

She glanced over to where her sisters were standing, then looked at him.

"For not asking me about…what happened earlier. With Scott. And for not letting him start anything. He wanted to make a scene, and I—couldn't—"

"It's okay."

She sighed. "People think he wants us to get back together, but he doesn't."

"I'm…sorry," Will said, for lack of anything better to say.

She shrugged. "Mostly, he just wants somebody to blame for what happened. Unfortunately for him, I wasn't the one with somebody on the side. Several 'somebodies,' actually. Well. Anyway. I really appreciate your help. He could have caused all kinds of trouble tonight, and Kate deserves better than that from me and what used to be mine."

Actually, Will thought that Arley had defused the situation—by walking away. She stood for a moment, seeming on the verge of saying something more, then decided against it.

"He's not still around someplace, is he?" Will asked, thinking she might be worried about running into him again.

"No. Gwen and Grace saw him leave." She glanced toward the sisters again. They looked no happier now than when Will had noticed them earlier.

A sudden cheer went up from the crowd as the car carrying the bride and groom moved a few inches.

"Arley! Arley, come here!"

The treelike sister had found her voice.

"Do you have any idea what it's like to have four mothers?" Arley asked him.

"Actually, I do," he said.

She turned to go, then didn't. "You aren't going to go off and do something…dangerous anytime soon, are you?"

"It's not in *my* plans."

"Are you afraid?" she asked bluntly. "Of being sent someplace…bad?"

"Sometimes."

They looked at each other—until she suddenly smiled again.

"Maybe we'll run into each other sometime—you can tell me about *your* mothers."

He didn't say anything, despite another opening she'd given him. But she didn't let his silence make her uncomfortable. She gave him a little wave and walked away. He watched her go, trying not to think about robots.

## Chapter Two

"Just who is that?" Grace asked, lowering her voice for once because of the crowd of people milling around them.

Arley looked steadily at both her sisters. Only Gwen seemed uncomfortable. Neither of them had the right to ask—especially Grace, whose own marriage had ended more abruptly than Arley's had. None of the sisters knew the reason for its sudden demise, and Grace apparently had no intention of enlightening any of them. She had an entirely different view of the right to privacy when *hers* was at stake. All Arley knew for certain was that Grace's husband had left, and Grace hardly seemed to notice.

At the moment, however, Arley had no desire to trade barbs about their assorted personal failures. For once, she opted to let the sisterly meddling slide.

Almost.

"You know, Grace, I'm getting a little tired of that question tonight," she said. "Did Scott put you up to it?"

"You don't even know that guy, Arley."

"Grace, I was only *talking* to him. I'm not taking him home with me. And I do know him. His name is Will Baron. He works with Kate. I ran into him once last summer. He was nice to Scottie, okay?"

"You're not that innocent," Grace said, and Arley laughed.

"You sound like a pop song lyric."

"You know how you are, Arley—and if you don't, *we* do. You're not trying to make Scott jealous with that soldier, are you?"

"Grace, please! I told you—we were just talking. He's an interesting person. He's from Arizona. He's half Navajo." She looked over her shoulder to where Will had been standing. He was no longer there.

"Well, Scott obviously didn't like it."

"What Scott likes or doesn't like is not my problem. Yours, either. He had no business being here in the first place."

"I said not to invite him," Gwen offered in spite of the look Grace gave her. "Nobody listened."

"He was *invited?*" Arley said incredulously, and several people turned to look in their direction.

"*I* invited him," Grace said. "To the reception. I was trying to head off trouble. It was purely a token gesture—a courtesy to our Scottie's father."

"Grace! Why didn't you tell me!"

"It was just a test, Arley! I didn't think he'd have the

nerve to actually show up. But he did, and now we know once and for all that he's—"

"This is none of your business, Grace!" Arley interrupted, as if that had ever deterred her oldest sister. Grace's determination was legendary in the family. It had probably cost her a husband, and it was about to cost her a sister, as well.

"It is if you don't have enough sense to realize he might use anything you do to try to get Scottie away from you."

"What?" Arley said, startled.

"You heard me. You know how Scott is, how his family is—or you should by now. I wouldn't put it past him or them. And he's not above doing something just to get back at you."

"How many times do I have to tell you? *I* didn't do anything wrong!"

"It doesn't matter if you did or didn't, Arley! That was then. I'm talking about right now. He's the kind of man who needs to save face. One of these days he's going to want to follow his grandfather and father into politics. He's going to need to trump that unfortunate adultery indiscretion. What better way than to try to prove you're an unfit mother and always were?"

Arley gave a sharp sigh. "I don't want to talk about this."

"You don't have to talk. Just listen for once. You never should have married Scott McGowan in the first place—but we got Scottie out of it, and I want us to keep him. Or would you rather his father had custody—in which case Scottie would probably grow up just like him."

"Grace, stop!" Gwen said, putting her hand on Grace's arm. "You're scaring her."

"I want to scare her."

Arley looked at both of them and shook her head.

"I'm not talking about this anymore," she said and walked away. She was too tired to battle Grace. Her head hurt. Her feet hurt. She just wanted to get her little boy and go back to Fayetteville.

"'Bye, Arley," Gwen called after her.

Arley waved her hand in the air to show she heard, not wanting to hurt Gwen's feelings just because she was upset with Grace. Grace could be annoying in the best of circumstances, more so when she was right. Scott McGowan wasn't above trying to get custody of Scottie—even if he *didn't* deserve it. He had made it his life's work to acquire things he didn't deserve—passing grades in college, business promotions, Arley Meehan. And he hadn't deserved her, not her love or her faithfulness or her willingness to believe in him far beyond what anyone with any sense would have done.

Even so, she could truthfully say that she hadn't been a complete idiot where Scott was concerned, regardless of what her sisters and everyone else might think. There was no denying that she had loved him, loved his wildness and his charm, so much so that she had been willing to ignore her growing lack of respect for him for a long time. But the day eventually came when she couldn't pretend anymore, when she couldn't let her emotions get dragged back and forth with every promise made and every promise broken. She had to walk away—for her son's sake, if nothing else. She had managed to do it—permanently—in spite of Scott's renewed "repentance" when he realized that, for once, he was going to suffer the consequences of his behavior.

"Arley!" someone called behind her—her uncle Patrick.

"You're not leaving already, are you—and without a goodbye for your old uncle?"

"I'm ready for hearth and home, Uncle Patrick."

"Well, I know the feeling. It was a fine wedding, wasn't it?"

"Yes," she said, feeling a ridiculous urge to cry.

"You hug that darling boy for me—and mind how you go."

"I'm a careful driver, Uncle Patrick."

"It's not the driving I was meaning."

She looked into his kind blue eyes. "*You've* been talking to Grace."

"Have not," he said. "I've been using my God-given eyes. And I'm not liking what I see, my girl. You and I both know Scott McGowan can get himself up to no good."

She sighed heavily. "Well, I am on the high side of suspicious," she said, and her uncle laughed.

"And that's a definite improvement—if you don't mind my saying so."

She didn't. The remark coming from him didn't bother her nearly as much as it would have if it had come from one of her sisters.

A large number of guests seemed to be making their way back into the pub.

"No rest for the wicked," Uncle Patrick said. "Are you sure you don't want to rejoin the festivities?"

"I'm sure. I'll bring Scottie to see you soon. He's got some new additions to his rock collection he wants to show you."

"The sooner, the better," he said, giving her one of his bear hugs, the kind that always made her feel better but this time brought her even closer to tears.

"Tell Grace and Gwen I've gone, if—when—they ask, will you?"

He looked at her a long moment. "I will."

She forced a smile and walked away. A group of soldiers walked ahead of her, laughing, talking and harassing each other the way soldiers always seemed to do. Will Baron wasn't among them. It annoyed Arley a great deal that Grace thought Arley might be using Will to get back at Scott. She wasn't. She just welcomed a little diversion. She was so tired of being worried and scared.

And lonely.

Scottie was nearly asleep when she picked him up at the great-aunts' house. He managed to walk to the car under his own power, but he was too sleepy to buckle himself into his safety seat.

"Mommy?" he murmured as she secured the belt and slipped his favorite pillow next to his head—a beagle dog pillow he'd named Dot, his threadbare sleeping, waking, stress and anxiety companion. She stood for a moment, then caressed his cheek before she closed the car door. There was nothing she wouldn't do for her son.

Nothing.

It began to rain when she was halfway home. She

drove carefully along the back roads leading to Fayetteville. Traffic was heavier than she expected. The coun-
tryside was illuminated by lightning from time to time,
but there were no strong winds or heavy downpours.
Scottie was afraid of thunder; she was glad he was
sleeping. He had too many things to be afraid of these
days, most of all that his father didn't love him. He was
so eager whenever Scott deigned to come around, trying
to impress him with his rock collection, his drawings
and papers from school, or how fast he could run and
how high he could jump—anything that might elicit
some indication that he had his father's undivided attention, just for a moment. That was sad enough, and what
was even sadder was that, for a time, Arley had been just
like him.

She was better now, though. Surprisingly better. Even
before the wedding reception, she had felt more comfortable about things than she had in a long time. All in
all, her life was going…reasonably well. She hadn't
caused any embarrassing moments for Kate—thanks to
Will Baron—and it was much more apparent to her now
that she was no longer afraid that she couldn't live
without Scott McGowan. Regardless of her sisters' misgivings, she was actually managing—except with
money. She needed a better and permanent job instead
of being sent pillar to post by the temp agency, and she
was going to keep taking courses at the community
college and filling out applications until she got one.

She smiled to herself. Scottie liked that; as soon as
school started, both of them would have to do
homework at the kitchen table.

Her mind suddenly wandered to the summer afternoon when she'd met Will Baron. She had hardly been at her best that day. She had been frantic to find Kate because of something Scott had or hadn't done, and because Scottie had misbehaved at the private kindergarten Scott was still paying for him to attend. She had felt totally overwhelmed by it all. She went looking for Kate at home and then at Mrs. Bee's house next door, and she found Will Baron in the sweltering upstairs hallway on an errand of his own. He may or may not have recognized the degree of her distress, but he had definitely recognized Scottie's. As they were leaving, he had taken a blue-green stone out of his pocket—a piece of turquoise—and had given it to Scottie for his collection.

He was kind to her son.

And that was the reason she remembered him. Yes, he was nice-looking. Yes, his eyes smiled long before his face did, and he smelled good. But it was because of Scottie that she'd asked Kate later about the paratrooper in Mrs. Bee's upstairs hallway. There was something intriguing about him, something that made her willing to brave Grace's criticism and the embarrassment Scott had caused her at the reception in order to talk to him again.

But that's all it was. A little conversation. She had told her sisters the truth when she said that Will Baron was an interesting person. He was, and it had been a long time since Arley had had any social interaction with anyone beyond her immediate family. There was no harm in it. None. The fact that Kate had invited him to the wedding in the first place should be recommendation enough for Gwen and the ever-suspicious Grace.

But Arley had no expectations that she would see Will Baron again. She rarely went on post—except for futile job interviews, and those were few and far between. She rarely went anywhere, for that matter, except to work at whatever paying position the temp agency found for her, and to the grocery store and to Scottie's school—and a fast-food restaurant as a treat for him as often as she could afford it. She had met Kate for lunch once or twice, taken Scottie to the post hospital, to the ward where Kate worked when the "get well" dogs were coming to visit, and she hadn't seen Will Baron any of those times. It wasn't likely that she'd run into him—unless she did something to make it happen. Which she wouldn't. She didn't need Grace's input to be concerned about Scott and his possible long-range plans where his son was concerned. It was just that Scottie had never been his priority—he thought nothing of skipping a visitation if it conflicted with his social plans—and she knew Scott McGowan well enough to know that actually *wanting* to be a real father might have nothing to do with his trying to get custody.

She reached to turn on the car radio for company. After a while, she drove out of a rain shower and then right back into another one—the story of her life, thus far. She didn't regret staying for the wedding reception, in spite of Grace's lecture and her skirmish with Scott. But if she wasn't careful, the reason she didn't regret it could become a full-blown family issue. The Meehan sisters tended to each other's business. She herself had been an all-too-willing participant in the Grace-led sister alliance to keep Kate from making what they had all thought was a huge mistake in becoming involved with a disabled paratrooper—a man younger than she was, no less. And Kate was considered the "sensible" one. Heaven only knew what would happen if it even looked like Arley the Handful might follow Kate's example with another member of the military, especially if it might cause problems with Scott.

But she was too tired to worry about it.

It was late when she finally arrived at her apartment, and it was still raining. As she carried the sleeping Scottie to the door, a white car she didn't recognize crept slowly past and turned around.

*Maybe we'll run into each other again.*

It wasn't an invitation. Will wasn't quite sure what it was—except another reason for his disharmony, which had more to do with his current state of mind than with the postwedding raucousness of the barracks tonight. Everybody was wound tight. Music seemed to be coming from behind every closed door, all of it different and all of it meant to effect the same end. He and his fellow soldiers were expecting to travel—sooner instead of later—and they were all looking for the right mind-set, the pumped-up killer high that would get them through it. He understood the dynamics perfectly. He'd never made a jump without doing the warrior chant all the way to the ground, in spite of his recent cynicism about following the Beauty Way.

He lay on his bed in the dark and tried to disengage himself from the thoughts swirling in his mind.

Harmony was essential for anyone who intended to follow Navajo teachings. If he were still a *hataalii*....

If.

He wasn't certain if the family knew that he'd all but lost the vocation he'd fought so hard for the privilege of learning. He had dedicated years of his life to becoming a Navajo healer, to learning the complexities of the mindset and the chants and rituals to achieve a kinship with Mother Earth and Father Sky. But what little "serenity" Arley had accused him of having completely eluded him now and had for a long time. He had had such big plans—once—assuming that he managed not to suffer any unfortunate consequences from being posted in harm's way and that his enlistment ended as scheduled. He was going to return to the reservation in triumph, where he would meld all the knowledge he had gleaned from both his worlds. He would use the medical skills he had acquired in the military to be a true help to Sloan, the aunt who had raised him and who was a nurse in the tribal health clinic, and he would continue to be a *hataalii*. He would skillfully practice both disciplines, all for the betterment of The People.

There had been a time when he'd been so sure, when he had actually thought that he could be both an army medic *and* a practitioner of the Navajo healing arts. He had told Arley the truth. He really could remember things—the chants and the details of the sand paintings necessary for the healing ceremonies with the precision the Holy People required. And he could remember all the medical procedures he'd been taught. He could even manage a high-powered weapon *and* urgent wound assessment on a computerized dummy in the dark and not let it go into cardiac arrest or bleed out. As far as he knew, no patient in either venue had ever suffered from a misstep that he could recall—except for the dummy, and that was early on. He had believed that all he had to do was not let himself get distracted. His desire to make all four of his "mothers" proud of him was strong, and so was his sense of obligation.

But somewhere he had lost his way, lost something integral he couldn't name; in the process, he had lost himself. He couldn't blame the army. He couldn't blame anyone. He had felt his sense of purpose and understanding, of belonging, slipping away from him long before he'd enlisted.

All he had left was a kind of perpetual discord in his heart and in his mind—and an unwelcome and unwise interest in Arley Meehan.

And he was definitely interested. He had been interested the first time he saw her, and he was still interested enough to want to go to a wedding on the outside chance that he would at least catch a glimpse of her, in spite of having no place in his disjointed life for personal involvements, especially the kind she represented. She had a child, and he was only passing through, regardless of his own tenuous family tie to the state. She was so pretty, so lively. Of all the guests at the wedding, *she* was the one he had wanted most to talk to, but it wasn't just that. She wasn't like anyone he had ever met. Aside from her obvious attributes, she was…astute. Right away, she had seen the advantage of his being posted in the state where the father he knew practically nothing about had been born. He doubted that anyone in his family had guessed that he had signed his enlistment papers thinking that he could eventually end up in central North Carolina.

He drew a sharp breath. If he were more like his half brother Patrick, he wouldn't let himself get all strung up in the reasons for, and the potential consequences of, his behavior. He would just go for it. He would see Arley Meehan as someone to help him pass the time—period. He would do something about it and not be concerned about anything but the pure pleasure of it.

But he wasn't like Patrick. He wasn't even like himself anymore.

*I don't know who the hell I am or where I belong,* he thought.

And he was running out of time to find out. He'd made all the arrangements he was supposed to make—his affairs were in order. When he'd been home last Christmas, he'd even allowed the Blessing Way to be performed on his behalf, an all-night Navajo ceremony that was supposed to make it possible for him to go to war with the blessing of the Holy People, even if he didn't actually believe in them anymore.

But he hadn't gone looking for the better understanding of his long-dead white father he used to think he wanted.

The Baron home place, the big house with a rambling front porch he knew only from photographs, still belonged to Sloan, and it was perpetually rented. He hadn't wanted to see it for the first time under those circumstances—with strange people living in it—or so he told himself. Besides that, it was located at the far end of his travel limit, and he had used that as an excuse, as well. Somebody in his squad would probably know a short cut, even if it involved driving through a surprised farmer's corn field, but he hadn't asked. Clearly, standing in the middle of his father's past in theory was very different from actually doing it. If he were completely honest, he would admit that he hadn't delved into the Baron family history because he was afraid to. He was unsettled enough as it was and not ready to find that his white heritage fit him no better than his Navajo heritage did.

A memory of Arley's young son suddenly came into his mind. He had immediately recognized the look in the boy's eyes. It came for being caught up in a whirlwind of uncontrollable adult events and being afraid to deal with it alone. He had seen the same expression all too often in the mirror when he was a boy, when Sloan and the tribe were squabbling over who he belonged to and who could raise him.

He sighed again in the dark. He had to stop thinking about Arley Meehan and her little boy and the problem she was apparently having with the man who had once been her husband. He had troubles of his own. He had to keep the family from worrying. It was natural that they would be worried about his likely imminent deployment, but they didn't know about his loss of direction. He'd told them nothing of his misgivings, and there was nothing he could do to reassure them.

*So how homesick are you?*

Maybe more than he had realized, he thought as he

felt his harmony dissipate even further in a sudden wave of longing for home. He missed his patched-up, mismatched family. He missed the desert, the place where he *almost* belonged. He missed…something unnameable, something a brief conversation with a pretty young woman had made him suddenly aware might be unavailable to him.

He took a quiet breath, trying to concentrate on the calm place deep inside him, the one he was only able to find after he had decided to be truly Navajo. The words of the *Hozhonji* song swirled in his mind. The song had great power. It spoke of helpmates and pairs and beauty.

The happiness of all things.

It was a blessing he would have said for Arley's sister and her new husband if the wedding had taken place in Window Rock instead of North Carolina, and if he were still himself.

*Maybe we'll run into each other again.*

## Chapter Three

"Have you called home in the last couple of weeks, E.T.?" Copus asked pointedly.

"Yeah," Will answered, getting better and better at deciphering Copus's science fiction analogies.

"Written any letters?"

"Yeah, why?"

"*Mailed* them?"

"Copus—"

"You're *sure* you haven't been neglecting the keeping-in-touch-with-the-family-in-a-timely-manner thing."

"I'm sure."

"Well, it ain't that, then."

"What are you talking about?"

"The lieutenant is looking for you, son," Copus said

ominously. "I got it straight from the horse's mouth—
a couple of stalls removed. Any minute now, he's going
to be wanting to see you ASAP."

Will accepted the prediction without comment. He
was mildly curious, but he kept stacking long packages
of unsterile 4x4 gauze on the supply closet shelf. The unit
phone was ringing in the background—making no impression whatsoever on the obviously non-busy Copus.

"Could I at least get a 'hooah' so I know you heard
me?" Copus said.

"Hooah."

"Son, how do you *do* that?" Copus asked.

"Do what?"

"*That.* Anybody else would be all over me wanting
to know what he wants. You don't even blink."

"I blink," Will said. He moved down to the next shelf
and continued restocking supplies.

"Yeah, but you don't ask."

"Not much point—since you don't know."

"Yeah, well, it just so happens, I got a theory or two.
And, lucky for you, I'm willing to share them. Assuming
that I'm handsomely rewarded for my trouble, of course."

"Forget it."

"No, now wait. See, I'm willing to help you out
here—get you prepared. But I got to have something for
my trouble."

Will glanced at him. Copus was ready to levitate off
the floor at the prospect of snagging a few bucks from
the unsuspecting but curious.

"No," Will said.

"Well, then, what do *you* think he wants?"

"Beats me."

"Could be he wants you to give him some pointers," Copus said.

"I don't have any pointers."

"Sure you do, son. You could tell him how to jump-start his love life." Copus grinned from ear to ear in appreciation of his own stellar wit and his not-so-subtle assessment of Will's nonexistent female conquests.

"If he wanted pointers for his love life, he'd be looking for you, not me," Will said.

"Then maybe you could give him some advice on how to live dangerously."

"He's in the army. He's probably already got that worked out."

Will moved to another shelf.

"Okay, William," Copus said. "You want to try to figure out what he wants or not?"

"Not," Will said without much hope.

"We could make a friendly little wager—how's about that?"

"Copus, I'm not losing what little money I've got on some dumb-ass bet."

"Okay, forget the bet. I think this is *big,* William. If it wasn't, one of the sergeants would be wanting to see you, not him. For some reason, you're on the fast track, son. I think you're going to want to get some kind of story worked out *before* you—"

"Copus!" someone yelled down the hall. Kate Meehan, now Doyle, had returned from her honeymoon and was in rare form.

"You'd think she'd be a in better mood," Copus said

under his breath. "Yes, ma'am!" he called, trotting off to see what she wanted.

Will continued restocking. He could hear Copus attributing his unfortunate lack of compliance to her will to circumstances beyond his control, specifically, his urgent need to find Specialist Baron on behalf of one Lieutenant Quinlan—who was not happy.

"I know all about the lieutenant's unhappy state. Baron!" she yelled. "Leave that and go see what he wants! And stop fiddling around!"

"He lives to serve," Copus said helpfully. "Fiddling around is not him."

"I meant *you,* Copus. Get busy!"

Will tried not to smile and went on his way, more than puzzled by the summons in spite of his outward nonchalance. He took the stairs instead of the elevator, and as he passed a row of windows on the ground floor, he realized it was raining again, a soft and steady "female" rain this time, instead of the usual summer thunderstorm. He was desert-raised, and the smell of it on dry earth was already in his mind. It wouldn't smell like that here, but it was still all he could do not to stop and simply admire it. He kept going until he reached the lion's den.

"The lieutenant wanted to see me," he told the only clerk he could find.

"He just left. He didn't say when he'd be back—but I'd wait around if I was you," he added when Will turned to go.

Will waited, watching the rain after all, amusing himself with visions of Copus having to take up the slack in his absence, however unlikely that might be.

About the time he decided to go back to the ward anyway, the lieutenant reappeared. Will could see immediately that Copus was correct in at least some of his estimation of the situation. The man was not happy. He looked as if someone had taken his harmony and drop-kicked it in front of a moving train.

"In!" he said sharply when the clerk advised him of Baron's presence, leading the way into his office. "Close the door."

"Sir, yes, sir," Will said.

"Sit."

Will sat.

The lieutenant plunked himself down behind the desk and carefully placed the stack of papers he was carrying on the desktop. "I'm not going to beat around the bush about this, Baron. We've had a complaint."

Will frowned slightly, rapidly trying to review the most recent aspects of his military life. Nothing came to mind that would cause his having to go straight to the assistant principal's office, once removed.

So he waited—one of the few military traditions which coincided with his own upbringing.

"Look. Specialist, you can *not*—I repeat, *not*—go around insinuating yourself into another man's marriage."

"Sir?" Will said, the unblinking state Copus admired so abruptly leaving him.

"Enough said?"

"Sir, no, sir. I don't understand—"

"Damn it, Baron, how much plainer can I get than that? Leave the woman alone!"

"Sir, what woman, sir?"

"How many damned married women are you chasing after?"

"Sir, none, sir."

The lieutenant gave a sharp sigh. "No? How about the one that fouled up the colonel's best golf game to date? He got a direct complaint from one of the civilians in his golfing party. This civilian says his son's estranged wife is getting herself tangled up with one of our own—a Specialist William Baron. That would be *you*. I understand there's a child involved, and as a result, the colonel would greatly appreciate it if you got your sorry ass out of the way of a family reconciliation—especially *this* family. Understood?"

"Sir, I'm not in anybody's way—"

"We're done here. Dismissed."

Will found Copus waiting to pounce on him the minute he exited the stairwell.

"Well?" Copus said, hurrying to keep up.

"You were right," Will said without stopping.

"I was? Damn. What was I right about? What?"

Will didn't answer him.

"What happened?"

"Nothing."

"So what did you do?"

"Nothing."

"Right. So what did you do?"

"I told you—nothing!"

But Copus wasn't about to give up. He trotted along, waiting for the big revelation—until he suddenly stopped. "No, you didn't!" he said loudly. "Tell me you didn't. Did you go messing around with you know who after what I told you?"

Will kept walking.

"Okay. You're not talking. I can respect that—and it ain't like that little flower ain't worth the picking—"

"I haven't been picking flowers!" Will said, causing several of their coworkers to stop what they were doing to listen.

"Well, it don't matter if you did or didn't—if *she's* what you got called in about, somebody's making damn sure you know the rules of engagement, son. I told you—didn't I tell you? You better start listening to your old Uncle Copus. So, are you going to tell her you got warned off her? Personally, I wouldn't advise it—"

"I don't even know her!"

"Yeah, but that didn't keep you from stepping up to the very real possibility of tossing her ex-husband on his ass at the wedding reception, now did it? So what are you going to do? What? What?"

"I'm going to mind my own business."

"Yeah, like that works."

"Specialist Copus!" Kate yelled down the hall. "What did I tell you?"

"Later, son," Copus said, drifting in the direction of where he was supposed to be. "And don't you worry. You and me are going to figure this thing out."

"What are you doing?"

Arley glanced at her third-oldest sister. There was just enough emphasis on the word *what* for her to realize that Kate didn't mean the cardboard box Arley

was packing in preparation for the move from the
current apartment she couldn't afford to the one Kate's
new husband had just vacated in the upstairs of Mrs.
Bee's big Victorian house. The Meehans had grown up
next door to Mrs. Bee, and Arley felt fortunate that
Mrs. Bee wanted her and Scottie as tenants. Arley was
very afraid suddenly that Kate was about to rain on her
parade.

"Maybe *you* better tell *me*," Arley said.

"Will Baron is a nice guy, Arley."

"Will Baron?" Arley said in surprise. "What about
Will?"

"You've put him in a bad situation."

"What are you talking about? I haven't seen him
since your wedding reception."

"Where he had some kind of altercation with
Scott—"

"That wasn't my fault! Grace is the one who invited
him. Maybe you ought to take whatever this is up with
her. And you owe Will Baron big-time, by the way.
Your reception could have turned into one big John
Wayne movie bar fight, if it wasn't for him."

"Never mind that. I understand Will got called in,"
Kate said.

"Kate, I don't know what that means."

"It means he had to go see his lieutenant, where it
was apparently suggested that he not associate with
you."

"What? Are you kidding me? Since when does the
army care if I talk to one of their medics for fifteen
minutes—tops?"

"I don't know the details, but I imagine the McGowans had something to do with it."

"What McGowans?"

"You know what McGowans."

"I don't know any McGowans with that kind of clout. Who told you all this—Will?"

"No. I heard it through the grapevine."

*Great,* Arley thought. *Two* sisters who speak in song lyrics.

"So it might not be true," she said, and Kate raised an eyebrow.

"Okay. Say it is true. You're telling me that some officer called Will in and told him not to have anything to do with me."

"I don't think he actually got lit up—"

"Oh, good," Arley said, completely mystified as to what that phrase meant, too.

"I imagine it was more a…suggestion," Kate said pointedly. "With these military types, sometimes it's hard to tell."

"Let me guess. The two can pretty much be the same thing."

"Pretty much."

"Kate, I am *not* going to believe the United States Army is run by the McGowan family. What are they going to do to Will if he talks to me again—put him in the brig?"

"That's the navy. But either way, public image is a lot more important to the military than it used to be. Believe me, an enlisted person's life is much less aggravating if his or her superior officers are happy and aren't made to look bad on the golf course."

"The golf course?" Arley said incredulously, and Kate shrugged.

"Will hasn't done anything except talk to me at the reception and keep Scott from trying to drag me outside when I didn't want to go. Oh, and last summer he gave Scottie a piece of turquoise for his rock collection. Now what is the problem with *that?*"

"I told you," Kate said. "Public image is a big deal, and who knows what spin the McGowans put on it. The alienation of affection law is still on the books in this state, you know."

"Well, this is just great. Did anybody happen to remember the divorce is final? Nobody is telling me who I can and can't talk to. Not the McGowans—and not the U.S. Army. And not anybody else, either!" she added.

"This isn't about you so much," Kate said in that quiet way she had when she was right and she knew it. "Will Baron shouldn't have to suffer the fallout because of your bad marriage, especially when he's just minding his own business."

"Well, gee, thanks, Kate. I really needed somebody to point that out. I'm already feeling like a big enough loser—and now I'm taking down the innocent bystanders."

"Arley, I just want you to get the big picture here."

"I got it! I have to get in touch with him."

"Who?"

"Will!"

"Did you hear what I just said?"

"Did you hear what *I* just said? I need to explain— to apologize."

"I don't think he'd want you to. I'm just telling you about this so you'll be forewarned. The McGowans have their connections, and they're not afraid to use them."

"Yeah, well, thanks for that, too. Hopefully, I can get *forewarned* every time I'm feeling the least bit good about things. And I know all about the McGowan 'connections.' It didn't matter to them one bit that Scott had sleazy women stashed all over town! All that mattered was that I looked the other way so their 'connections' wouldn't be forced to witness an ugly divorce!"

"Hey! This is not my fault!"

"I know that! You're just…the only one here."

Kate smiled and gave her a quick hug. "I've got to go. I'm glad you're moving almost home again. It'll be nice having you and Scottie at Mrs. Bee's."

"Does Grace know about this thing with Will?"

"No-o-o-o," Kate assured her. She gave her a peck on the cheek and left.

Arley stood staring at the cardboard box she'd been packing. She could try calling the hospital. She could leave a message for Will to call her. That would be easy enough. Or…

It occurred to her as her initial aggravation subsided that she was so used to the McGowan way, she wasn't really all that surprised. They had their prejudices, not the least of which was their disdain for all things military, despite owing a good deal of their fortune to the proximity and spending power of the United States Army. But, for once, Arley decided she wasn't going to

## Chapter Four

"**Y**ou still here, Baron? Somebody was at the nursing station looking for you."

Will looked up from the dressing he was changing. The message-bearer was one of the more mobile soldiers on the unit who entertained himself by rolling up and down the hall in a wheelchair all day gathering intelligence. At the moment he was working to get his chair to make a sharp U-turn so he could stop in the doorway.

"Who is it?" Will asked, but he was thinking, "Now what?"

"Don't know," the intelligence-gatherer said. "I just heard them trying to decide if you were still here or not."

Will gave a quiet sigh and finished securing his

patient's fresh stump bandage in place, his mild pleasure that his workday might actually conclude without incident dissipating. He had no real reason to expect the worse—except for the way things had been going lately. Clearly, Coyote, the Navajo mischief-maker, functioned just as well here as he did on the reservation in Arizona, whether anybody believed in him or not.

"Okay, buddy," he said to his patient. "You're good to roll."

"Thanks, man. It was getting pretty rank."

Will stood back so the soldier could maneuver back into his wheelchair without any unwelcome help, then he cleaned up the area and walked into the corridor past the open doors and through the usual hospital din of miscellaneous television programs, conversations and music.

And a dog barking as quietly as a dog knew how, apparently on cue.

He'd forgotten the dogs were visiting the unit today. He stopped to let a portable X-ray machine roll out of one of the patient rooms, then continued toward the nurses' station.

He saw Arley first, then the tall red-haired man standing close by.

"Patrick!" he said in disbelief.

"Hey, poco bro," Patrick said, stepping forward and executing the male clasping-of-right-hands, inside-shoulder-bump greeting with ease. "Long time, no see."

"What are you doing here?" Will said, still incredulous at finding him on post, of all places. "Is everybody okay?" He hadn't heard anything good or bad about

Patrick in weeks, except that nobody in the family knew where he was—again. Patrick never called or wrote letters. He just showed up—but in Window Rock, not on the other side of the country.

"Everybody's fine. I came to see you, bro—he's a good brother, but he's not all that bright," Patrick added to Arley, and she smiled. Clearly, he'd made her acquaintance while he was waiting.

"It's—I'm…surprised," Will said. The impact of seeing both Arley and Patrick where he didn't expect to find either of them had left him speechless. He glanced at her. She was wearing a white sundress with yellow buttons, and she looked…so good. He'd forgotten how pretty she was, how…everything.

"So! Patrick! How long are you going to be here?" he asked his brother abruptly, forcing himself to look away from Arley. Patrick was wearing the expensive turquoise-and-silver cuff bracelet their uncle by marriage had had made for him years ago—a good sign that Patrick had a cash flow of sorts and hadn't been forced to pawn it again.

"That would be hard to say," Patrick said unhelpfully. He was trying not to grin, clearly enjoying himself for reasons Will had yet to determine. But then Patrick *always* enjoyed himself, even when he was sober.

But, as glad as Will was to see him, his focus was still on Arley.

"Are you looking for Kate?" he asked her.

"Well, no. It's…I'm…"

"Ready to go when you are, bro," Patrick interrupted. "You get to pick the restaurant—I'm buying."

Will glanced at Arley again. She seemed about to say something more, but didn't.

"Nice to meet you, Arley," Patrick said to her, steering her attention in his direction. "Thanks for keeping me company."

"It was nice to meet you, too."

It should have been their cue to leave, but Patrick stood a moment longer.

"'Bye, Will," Arley said and walked away.

He could feel Patrick looking at him, in a way that made him think his irrepressible half brother was on the verge of making some pithy remark.

But Patrick didn't say anything, and he continued *not* saying anything all the way to the elevators and out of the hospital. He remained silent as they walked to where Patrick had parked his truck.

"What!" Will said finally when he couldn't take it any longer.

"You working at the hospital tomorrow?" Patrick asked mildly, as if he'd been waiting for just such an opening.

"Yeah," Will said cautiously.

"Day or evening?"

"Evening. Seven to seven. If not longer."

"Good. No reason why we can't visit *and* carry furniture."

"What are you talking about?"

"She's moving—Arley. I said we'd help."

"I can't help her move."

"Sure you can."

"No, I can't."

"Why not?"

Will didn't answer him. He was perfectly aware that it wasn't because of a conversation between a couple of high-powered men on a golf course that he was refusing. It was because of how much he wanted to help her—and he wasn't about to share that with his uncontainable brother.

"Look, bro. Her sister's husband can't do much carrying yet and everybody else they know with any muscle is either working or gone to the beach. We move a little furniture, maybe we get a beer out if it. No big deal, right?"

"Wrong."

Patrick stared at him. "Okay," he said after a moment. "My mistake."

"Where—?" Will said when they reached Patrick's beat-up truck—which was in approximately in the same rattletrap condition on the outside as the one Will drove. If they put the best parts of both of them together, they still wouldn't have a decent-looking vehicle.

"Where what?" Patrick asked when Will didn't go on.

"Where…is she moving?"

"What do you care?" Patrick said, grinning. "You can't help."

"Damn it, Patrick, where is she going?"

"She's going to a Mrs. B's house. I don't know what the *B* stands for."

"That's her name. B-e-e," Will said, far more relieved than he should have been that she wasn't leaving town.

"You know Mrs. B-e-e?"

"Yeah, I know her."

"You know Miss Arley pretty well, too, huh?"

"I…know her. Barely."

"Uh-huh. That's what I thought. *Barely*—because nobody in Window Rock ever heard of her. Imagine my surprise when I found out she and I were waiting to see the same Specialist Baron."

"What?"

"You heard me."

"She was waiting to see me?"

"That's what she said."

"She didn't say anything."

"No, she didn't, did she? That's all right, though. You can find out what she wants tomorrow. Oh, I forgot. You're not helping. You know, for somebody you *barely* know, she didn't bat an eye when I said I was your brother. Most people look at least a little surprised—I think it must be the red hair," Patrick added with a grin. "Not our Miss Arley, though. I would have bet money she already knew a few things about Specialist Will Baron and his unusual family tree."

"I told her I had a half brother," Will admitted. "I didn't say he was redheaded and butt-ugly."

Patrick punched him on the arm—hard.

"You still hit like a girl," Will said, and they both laughed.

"I'm glad to see you, bro," Patrick said after a moment.

"Did Sloan send you?" Will asked, thinking their aunt's hand must be somewhere in Patrick's sudden, unprecedented urge to drive a couple thousand miles to visit.

"She's…concerned," Patrick said.

"About what?"

"She thinks you're off the path."

Will made no comment. Sloan Baron-Singer, their father's only sister, had been born and raised not far from here. She didn't—couldn't—really understand the Navajo concept of walking in beauty, regardless of the fact that she'd lived on the rez since Will was three. She did, however, understand the boys she'd guided into manhood—both of them.

"So I figured we could hang out for a while—raise a little hell," Patrick said. "And then I'll tell her you're fine. You *are* fine, right?"

"Yeah," Will said. "I'm fine."

"You just dropped the ball for a minute there, I guess."

"What is that supposed to mean?"

"It means you forgot the honored teachings from both sides of the family. You know—the Southern no-staring thing, and the Navajo watch-the-eye-contact thing? Obviously you were wanting to drag Miss Arley off someplace and have your way with her."

"Patrick—"

"Don't worry, bro. I'm not going to tell the folks in Window Rock you've been running around *looking* at people—especially girl people you barely know."

"I'm not going to help her move."

"Then you can give me directions to Mrs. Bee's house and I'll help her. I understand you know the way. Hey," he said, apparently because of the look on Will's face, "it's no big deal. I'll just have to carry enough for the two of us."

Will tried to believe that, all through their boisterous

dinner at the Steak and Ale, where Patrick entertained every waitress who wandered by their table, and then later when they were back at Patrick's budget motel on the outskirts of town. Will was still hopeful the next morning when he woke up. Somebody's radio was playing "I Want To Be Your Man"—which echoed in his mind throughout his entire early-morning run. The hope that he could rely on Patrick to do what he said he would do completely evaporated when Will was met in the barracks hallway by a determined-looking Copus.

"Got something for you, son," Copus said, looking down at the pink slip of paper in his hand.

"What is it?" Will said, reaching out to take it.

"Now, wait a minute. I didn't take the message and Trask writes like a drunk chicken on roller skates. Let me figure this out—oh, okay," he decided, turning the paper around. "He said…"

"Who said?"

"Your brother…?"

"Patrick."

"Yeah, Patrick. He said to tell you he'd been in an all-night poker game—I like him already," Copus said as an aside. "And…what with driving cross-country *and* staying up late talking to you—not to mention the poker playing—he's got to crash now or die, and he can't help with the moving this morning—who's moving?"

"What else?" Will said, not about to tell him.

"That's it. Oh, no," Copus said, turning the pink slip over. "He says he needs some money."

"Great," Will said under his breath.

"Reckon how he found a poker game so fast?" Copus said.

"If finding a poker game was a paying job, my brother would be Donald Trump," Will said.

"Like I said. I like him already."

Copus handed him the pink slip, and Will stood there looking at it, seeing nothing. He was under no obligation whatsoever to meet Patrick's verbal commitment to carry furniture. None.

He gave a heavy sigh and walked outside anyway, leaving Copus with his curiosity. Some things never changed. Will was the Baron family peacemaker, mediator, facilitator, *and* the saver of faces. And, for some reason, Sloan had sent Patrick here to take care of *him*. He wondered if she had forgotten what a burden Patrick could be.

No. Not likely, he decided. Patrick and his total disregard for consequences had nearly cost her custody of Will after his father died. And yet Patrick was the one who had rescued him when Will's birth mother had kidnapped him from the children's receiving home—not because she wanted him, but because she wanted to matter. Will could still remember the secluded, ramshackle trailer where she'd hidden him, how afraid he had been—of her and of the drunken man she lived with. He'd been too afraid to cry, to eat, to sleep. And then he'd looked up and seen Patrick and Meggie's not-yet-husband, Jack Begaye, lying in wait in the underbrush. Patrick, his incredible, redheaded big brother, had come running as hard and fast as he could in spite of the boyfriend with the shotgun, stealing Will right out from under the boyfriend's and Margaret Madman's noses. Patrick had brought Will, albeit sick and feverish, safely home again. It was Patrick who had read "Goodnight Moon" aloud a hundred times during Will's convalescence and offered his hand for holding so Will could dare to sleep.

Which was one of the reasons why Will got into his own beat-up truck now and headed to Mrs. Bee's house. It was early still, and it was already hot. He was sweaty from his run, thirsty and still a long way from finding his harmony.

He parked in front of the big Victorian house that reminded him a little of the Baron home place, which he'd seen in a photo Sloan had given him. He didn't see anyone around. He stood outside the truck for a moment, then headed for the picnic table under one of the big shade trees in the backyard to wait. There was a slight breeze in spite of the heat, and someone had planted a well-tended garden nearby. He stood watching the bees work their way through an assortment of tomato and cucumber and squash blossoms. He could hear a radio playing somewhere and the rolling rattle of what he guessed was some beat-the-heat skateboarding going on somewhere down the street. Beads of sweat rolled down his face, and he wiped them away with the tail of his T-shirt.

"Hey," a voice said behind him.

He looked around to find Arley standing a few feet away. She was wearing shorts and a midriff-baring top that had little ribbon bows on it, and she looked as hot and sweaty as he did—only she was beautiful. If there had been any doubt in his mind, his immediate visceral response to seeing her underlined that there was no way he could pretend he was here solely to keep Patrick's word for him. Finding her like this and talking to her again were the reasons, and maybe they both knew it.

"Where's Patrick?" she said.

"Patrick is…there was an all-night poker game," Will said in explanation.

Arley smiled. "He wasn't kidding, then."

"About what?"

"He said he was the black sheep of the family."

Will looked toward Mrs. Bee's house. He could hear the banging of pots and pans through the open kitchen window and someone singing "Blessed Assurance."

"So…Patrick is all about poker games," Arley said when he looked at her again.

"No, Patrick is all about burning the candle at both ends, knowing it's dangerous, and still admiring the light."

"And you watch his back while he's burning." It wasn't a question.

"Not so much anymore. Hey, you're not the one who told him about the poker game, are you?"

She laughed softly. "Not guilty," she said. "For once. I didn't recommend any topless bars, either." She pushed a tendril of hair that had fallen into her eyes behind her left ear. In spite of his upbringing, he watched the journey and the ultimate destination.

She looked around as a small white car drove slowly past Mrs. Bee's house.

"I may be more in need of one of your other relatives," she said, watching it go down the street, turn around and come back.

"Who?"

"The kick-butt lawyer—"

The screen door slammed at the house next door, and Arley's unbending sister came striding across the backyard.

"Arley! We should have gone with them!" she called, ignoring Will. "It's taking too long!"

"No, we shouldn't. We have to make room to put the stuff they're bringing. Kate would call if they needed help."

"They've got *Gwen* with them, Arley. Who knows what she'll get herself into. I still say—"

"Grace, this is Specialist Will Baron," Arley interrupted. "Will, this is my oldest sister, Grace."

"Has he come to help?" Grace asked before he could respond—as if he weren't standing there.

"Yes, ma'am. I have," Will said.

"Then why isn't he helping?" she asked, still ignoring him while he suppressed a smile. He had grown up surrounded by strong women, and he'd always enjoyed the way their minds worked.

"What can I do?" he asked.

"Those boxes on the porch need to be carried upstairs," Arley said, beating Grace to any plans she might have.

"Okay. Nice to meet you, ma'am," Will said to Grace. She didn't say anything, but clearly the feeling wasn't mutual.

\* \* \*

Arley lost her nerve. She had intended to apologize to Will for putting him in an awkward position with his superiors even if he wasn't "lit up." But, she didn't do it, in spite of her earlier decision that this was one apology she really ought to make. Kate was right. Will Baron shouldn't have to suffer for Arley's bad marriage.

She followed him toward the porch until her shoelace came untied, then she bent down to retie it. When she stood up, she realized that the same white car she'd just seen was cruising past again.

Someone could be looking for a particular house, she thought.

Or someone could be looking to see if she was consorting with a paratrooper. Unfortunately, given recent events, she considered one scenario as likely as the other, especially since lately there seemed to be a number of unidentified cars gliding past her places of residence.

She gave a quiet sigh. Dealing with Scott McGowan was like dealing with a whirlwind. He disrupted everything and then moved blithely on. He had Scottie this weekend and, surprisingly, he hadn't backed out at the last minute, even knowing she was moving. If these cruising cars did have something to do with Scott, then she should tell Will to leave right now, say she had everything under control, and she didn't need his help. She should call to him, apologize for the trouble she'd caused him, say thank you very much and send him on his way. She should *not* take any chances where her underhanded ex-husband was concerned—except that this didn't feel risky. It felt like a pleasant way to get through an overwhelming task.

She continued to watch as Will propped the screen door open with one box and carried in another, then she followed him into the house.

She stayed in the foyer because she kept expecting Grace to jump on her broom, circle the house a few times, and then come to deliver one of her all-too-familiar tirades. But, for once, Grace stayed right where she was. Standing in the yard, looking exasperated.

Arley waited a moment longer, then went upstairs. There was no reason why Will's presence should be viewed as some kind of "situation," and she really could use the help.

"What's the plan?" he asked when he saw her.

"I want to move Scottie's things into his room—in there," she said. "His name is on the boxes."

"I got it," he said, when they both reached for the same box.

She stepped back and let him take it, then began moving the kitchen boxes into a stack in front of the small electric range.

She glanced at him from time to time, looking for some sign that he was worried about being here or feeling put upon. If he wanted to leave, she couldn't tell it by looking.

She turned on the radio and tuned it to the first station she came to, trying to focus on the music instead of the growing realization of how glad she was that Will Baron was here.

"So tell me," she said abruptly.

"Tell you what?" he asked, lifting another box and moving it into Scottie's small room.

"Anything. This is an open forum."

"You first," he said.

He was such a challenge, she thought, trying not to smile, and he didn't even know it.

"Okay. Scottie still has that piece of turquoise you gave him. He calls it his blue sky rock. He says the little gray veins in it are baby rain clouds, waiting to get big enough to make a big storm."

Will smiled, but he didn't say anything.

"Your turn," Arley said pointedly. She followed him into Scottie's room and opened one of the "Scottie" boxes to empty it. It was full of little-boy clothes. She took out a stack of T-shirts and began putting them into dresser drawers. "Let's hear something about your part of Arizona."

"There's a monsoon season—when it rains," he said without hesitation.

"There is? I didn't know that," she said truthfully. "What else?"

"The Navajo tribe is a matriarchy. The women own the property—traditionally speaking, that is."

"I didn't know that, either," she said. "Go on. Don't stop now."

"I…used to be a *hataalii*," he said after a moment.

"Why aren't you still one?" she asked, specifically because she thought he expected her to be logical and ask for a definition of the word. She looked up in time to see the expression that passed over his face.

"Why aren't you still one," she asked again, serious this time, letting go of her bantering attitude.

"I'm not sure," he said.

"How hard is it to be a...?"

"*Hataalii*. Pretty hard," he said.

"And harder to stay one, I guess."

"Maybe not for some."

"What does a *hataalii* do, exactly?" she asked, still putting away Scottie's clothes. She glanced at him. He was trying to decide if he wanted to tell her.

She waited.

"Healing ceremonies," he said finally. "With sand paintings."

"Like a medicine man?"

"Something like that."

"Did the army make you give it up?" she asked, because that seemed a real possibility given the meddling the military was apparently doing in *her* life.

"No. You have to have real harmony to do it. I was losing mine before I enlisted."

"Maybe you can get it back."

"I don't think so. I'm on my way to the sandbox."

She didn't know exactly what that meant, but she understood it wasn't desirable.

"Keep going," she said. "Ask a question this time."

"Are you getting back with your husband?" he asked, and there it was: everything on the table. She had the impression that the question surprised him as much as it did her.

They looked at each other across the boxes. "Green-eyed Lady" was playing on the radio and downstairs

Mrs. Bee was still singing her way through the Cokesbury Hymnal.

"No," she said evenly. "I'm not. The divorce is final and it's taken me a long time to get to where I am now. No," she said again.

Arley abruptly went back to emptying the box. "I was wondering…" She looked up, and he was waiting for her to finish the sentence.

"I was wondering," she began again, "if you wanted to come to dinner—with Scottie and me—as a thank-you for helping us move."

"I…"

"I'd like for you to," she said before he could decline. "If you want to, that is," she added.

*And if he didn't mind risking that "lit up" thing again.*

"Okay," he said, more to her vicinity than to her.

She smiled. He did that sometimes, she realized. He didn't quite look at her, which caused much more of an impact when he ultimately did.

"Okay. I'll call you when I get settled—I think your number's on Mrs. Bee's phone bulletin board downstairs. I guess from when you were helping Cal get to his clinic appointments. Unless it's changed."

"No."

"I should warn you, though. I can't cook anything but Tar Heel cuisine."

"Fine by me."

"You don't even know what that is."

"Sure I do. We had Tar Heel cuisine every time one of the Carolina family members got homesick. I even like it."

"Hey."

They both looked around. Patrick Baron stood in the open doorway, and Arley had no trouble believing he'd been playing poker all night.

"I thought you were going to crash?" Will said.

"So did I," Patrick said. "Couldn't sleep. Arley! We meet again," he said to her, his considerable charm intact, in spite of the obvious sleep deprivation. "Sorry I didn't make it sooner. I met your sister Grace on the way in—I thought she was going to frisk me. She's cute, though—you can tell her I said that, but wait until after I leave. Will, I need to talk to you a minute—outside."

Arley waited a moment after they walked downstairs, then slid a box across the room to an open space under one of the double windows just so she could see where they were going, although it was none of her business. They walked across the yard to where Patrick had parked his truck. She didn't see Grace anywhere— which was probably a good thing.

The windows were open, but she couldn't hear their conversation. She could only see Will take out his wallet and give his brother money. She could also see a car pull up, one she recognized.

"Oh, now what?" she said, turning and running down the stairs two at a time to intercept Scott as he walked across the front yard. She could tell by the look on his face that he intended to accost the Baron brothers.

"What is it, Scott?" she called to him. She made no attempt to introduce him. He already knew who Will was, and he could just guess about Patrick.

"I need that stupid dog pillow," Scott said. "I don't know why you let Scottie have that thing."

"He must have left it in the car," she said, surprised because she was certain Scottie had put it in his backpack. "And I let him have it because he loves it and needs it."

"Yeah, it's so important you forgot to make sure he had it with him," he said. And then he smiled.

"Well, I do have a lot of things on my mind today," Arley said.

"I can see that," he said, glancing at Will.

Arley bit back the retort he was trying so hard to get her to provoke. She walked to her car instead to look for the dog pillow. It wasn't there.

"I'll check the apartment again. I thought it was in his backpack."

"No, Arley, it isn't."

"Then I'll look for it. If I find it, I'll bring it by," she said.

"Maybe I'll just let it stay lost," Scott said. "Wean him off it cold turkey."

"Don't do that, Scott."

He smiled again, and it took everything she had not to say more. She stood, waiting for him to get into his car and drive away, realizing suddenly that Scottie's pillow likely wasn't lost at all. Scott had come for a firsthand look at who was here.

"Nice guy," she heard Patrick say behind her.

## Chapter Five

The drunken chicken on roller skates had been taking messages again. Will saw the pink slip taped to his door as soon as he dragged his extremely filthy, banged-up body out of the stairwell and into the hallway. Concentrating on keeping his macho image intact, while not aggravating his many blisters, bruises, scrapes and bug bites, he made his way to his door—without limping—and tore off the pink slip. Reading it was something else again.

"Damn, Baron, what happened to you—you burn in?"

Will ignored the passing soldier's question regarding the possibility that his parachute hadn't opened and tried to decipher the message. It didn't come from Arley. Her name wasn't anywhere on it, and his disappointment was considerable.

The words looked like *Toddy drummer al 7. Cave ef coul cone.* There was no return phone number.

He tried looking at the message from another angle, but it didn't help. Neither did having been sleepless and in simulated warfare for days. The only person who might be able to decipher it—besides the chicken himself—was Copus, and Will wasn't about to go to him for assistance.

He looked at the slip one more time before he declared it totally beyond his capabilities and stuck it in his pocket. Despite his exhaustion and pain, it only took him a moment to formulate a Plan B. He'd take a shower, work on the places that hurt the worst, eat, sleep a couple of hours, and then he'd worry about what the pink slip said. After he ate some more.

He sincerely hoped that Patrick had been behaving and that the message didn't have anything to do with him. But Will had been gone nearly two weeks, and he didn't even know if Patrick was still in the state. If he was, Will doubted Patrick was gambling again, mostly because he didn't have enough money to get into another poker game. Or, more precisely, Will didn't have enough money to give him to get into another poker game.

He let himself into his quarters, planning to head for the shower. He meant to wash off the dirt, but he didn't make it past his bed. He fell across it and closed his eyes. When he opened them again, he had no idea what time it was or how long he'd been there. He hoped it was the same day.

He forced himself up, staggering into the kitchen he shared with another soldier he had yet to meet, a medic on hardship leave because of some pressing family trouble. He looked in the refrigerator out of habit, not because he expected to find anything edible, then he picked up his truck keys and wallet and headed out, noting as he left that there were no more pink slips taped to the door.

"You better saddle up, man," someone said behind him—Trask, the official barracks message-taker.

"What are you talking about?"

"I'm talking about the cute-sounding girl who called. Don't you bother reading your messages either? I know you never check to see if you've got any. I put it on the damn door so you'd see it."

"I couldn't read the thing! What did it say?"

"What am I, The Amazing Kreskin? You're not the only one who gets phone calls, you know—okay, okay," Trask said when Will took a step toward him. "It was a girl, she sounded hot, she said to tell you, 'Today, dinner at seven. Call if you can't come.' Or something like that."

"Seven," Will said.

"That's what she said—I could have put 1900 hours, but I'm very exact. What they say is what you get. You look kind of rough, dude. I think I'd call her and re-schedule if I was you."

"You didn't put a phone number on it!"

"Sure I did—well, maybe not," he decided, apparently because of the look Will gave him.

Seven.

Will looked at his watch. Twenty minutes from now.

"Trask," he said. "You should know, when I get back, I'm probably going to kill you."

"I'll put it in my day planner," Trask said, unimpressed.

Will tried calling Arley via Mrs. Bee's phone number, but no one answered. He had no choice but to scrape as much dirt off himself as he could and hobble out. As it was, he arrived at Mrs. Bee's house twenty-two minutes late. He was reasonably clean, but that was the most he could say for himself. Basically, he looked—and felt—as if he'd been thrown off his horse in the middle of a cattle stampede.

Arley's car wasn't in the driveway. Neither was the vintage vehicle he'd seen parked in Mrs. Bee's aged, unattached garage.

With considerable effort, he walked up the steps to the back door and rang the bell. No one answered. He stood for a moment, then walked into the backyard. It was hard not to hobble.

He made his way to the picnic table and sat down—painfully—to review his options. Wait or leave. He decided to wait.

Eventually, a small silver car turned into the driveway and stopped. The back door opened, and Scottie got out. There was something wrong. Will realized it the moment he saw the boy's face. And he wasn't with Arley; he was with his lovable aunt Grace.

Scottie waited for her to get out of the car, then stood for a moment looking up at her before he walked with her to where Will was sitting.

The dog pillow had been located, Will saw as they approached. Scottie had it clutched tightly to his chest.

"What are you doing here?" Grace asked bluntly.

"I'm waiting for Arley," Will said. He had no idea whether or not Grace actually knew he'd been invited for dinner and if not, he didn't want to be the one to break the news to her.

"She's not here—and she's not going to be here— for a while," she added quickly, because the remark clearly alarmed her nephew.

"Hey, Scottie," Will said. "How's the rock collection coming?"

"Good," Scottie said, but his voice trembled and he kept looking at his aunt.

"Your mom told me you still had your blue sky rock."

The boy nodded.

"I see you found your pillow."

Will realized immediately that that was the wrong thing to say. Scottie suddenly bowed his head. He made no sound, but the tears spilled down his cheeks. Will looked at Grace, who seemed as distressed as the boy.

Ignoring his aches and pains, Will slid closer to Scottie. "What's the matter, Scottie?" he asked the boy gently.

"I can't—fix her," he thought Scottie said.

"What? The pillow?"

"Dot," Scottie said, looking at him now. He turned the pillow so Will could see. There appeared to be a significant tear in the fabric on the front side, from the dog's chin down to its chest, and the stuffing was spilling out.

"Scottie, honey," Grace said. "We can sew it—or we'll get you another one. It's—"

From the look on the boy's face neither option was acceptable.

"How about I take a look at her?" Will said. "I'm

pretty good at fixing soldiers when they get hurt. Maybe I can do something to fix Dot. Okay?"

Scottie looked at him doubtfully, then allowed Will to inspect the tear.

"She needs suturing. I can do it—but I'd need you to help," Will said.

"Okay," Scottie said, his voice still shaky.

"Good. Any chance of finding something to suture with?" he asked Grace, hoping she wouldn't mention "sewing" again. "It would involve thread and—"

"I *know* what suturing is."

"And we need some kind of bandage."

Grace raised both eyebrows. "Bandage," she repeated.

"Yes, ma'am," Will said.

She gave a short exhalation of breath. "I'll be right back."

She went to the house next door and let herself in with a key. While she was gone, Will had Scottie put Dot on the picnic table. He laid her down carefully, but more of the tiny Styrofoam pellets spilled out of the rip in the dog print fabric. Will helped Scottie put back as much as they could.

"I don't want to throw her in the trash," Scottie said after a moment. "My dad said she was making a big mess."

"Don't worry. I think we can take care of that."

Grace was back—with several needles already threaded with black thread, a pair of scissors, a pair of tweezers, and a handful of adhesive bandages with cartoon characters on them.

"Outstanding," Will said. "You ready?" he asked Scottie.

The boy nodded.

"Okay. You hold the scissors and the tweezers for me. Grace, you can open some of those bandages. Three should do it. Scottie, you pick which ones you want."

By the time the bandage selection had been made and readied, Will had the tear sewn up. "Scissors," he told Scottie, who handed them over with authority. "Okay. Now you can stick the bandages on—what do you think?"

"Looks…good," Scottie decided.

"It'll be like a scar," Will said, "but her stuffing will stay in." He gave Grace her improvised medical supplies back. She still looked as if she might turn him into a frog.

"You think this is going to get you brownie points with my sister, don't you?" she asked the minute Scottie took Dot and trotted off to play.

He ignored the question and asked one of his own. "Where's Arley?"

"The last time I saw her, she—" Grace stopped and looked up at the sky, then at him. "She was having a…discussion with Scott. About the dog pillow. She called me and asked me to come get Scottie and wait here until she gets back. She didn't mention anything about you. Whatever plans the two of you had, believe me, they're off."

"I believe you," he said. "But I think I'll hang around for a while anyway."

"I don't think that's a good idea."

"Look, Grace, I'm not planning to add to Arley's problems."

"Well, you will. You *are*. Scott McGowan is—"

They both looked around as Arley's car pulled into the drive and over to the side so as not to block Grace's exit. She sat for a moment before she got out.

"Mom, look!" Scottie called to her, holding up Dot. "She got, she got…what is it?" he called to Will.

"Sutured," Will said.

"She got sutured," Scottie said.

"Well, look at that," Arley said. "Good as new and then some. Hey," she said to Will as she walked up. She frowned suddenly. "What happened to you?"

"Field training exercises," he said. "I'm supposed to look like this."

"Well, that's a relief. I thought maybe Grace had done it—or you'd been to one of Patrick's all-night poker games. Grace, thanks for bringing Scottie home."

"You're welcome," Grace said. "Arley, are you sure this is a good—"

"*Goodbye,* Grace. Thanks again. Really."

Grace made a small sound of disapproval and walked away.

Arley waited until Grace had gotten into her car and was backing out the driveway. "I'm glad you could make it," she said, turning her attention to him. "Are you sure you're okay?"

"Yeah. I'm good to go—but if you want to put this off, it's okay."

"Why would I want to do that?"

Will didn't say anything.

"Oh. Grace told you Scott and I had words. Well, we did and it's nothing new. You're here, I'm here. Dot is 'sutured' and I'm ready to get cooking. Dinner will be a little later than I'd planned, but other than that, all's right with the world—if we don't count the way you look. Are you sure you're…good to go?"

"Yeah."

"Maybe you better define *good.*"

"Well, my chute opened. I didn't get struck by lightning. I didn't get run over by anything bigger than a guy running from a snake."

"You still look pitiful."

"I'm doing the best I can," he assured her, and she laughed.

"Okay. If you say so."

He got up from the picnic table bench almost without wincing, and they walked together toward the house. He had to work hard not to limp.

"Look at you," she said in spite of his efforts. "And here I was hoping to go dancing."

"I can dance," he assured her. "Or I could if I knew how."

She picked up his hand and put it on her shoulder so he could use her for a walking cane of sorts. He found it helpful and pleasant. Very pleasant, actually.

"Cal and Kate used to walk around like this all the time," she said. "It must go with paratrooper territory. Are you hungry?"

"Beyond hungry," he said truthfully.

"Good. Are you worried I can't cook?"

"No—that's how hungry I am."

She laughed again, and Scottie stopped playing "Dot, the Airplane" long enough to hold the screen door for them to go inside.

"Thanks, buddy," Will said.

"You're welcome," he said, then darted around them to race up the stairs to the apartment.

Will made it up the many steps without Arley's help. She walked ahead of him to open the apartment door, and he used the opportunity to appreciate the fine shape of her legs.

Very fine.

She was wearing some sort of high-heeled, backless shoes. All women should wear high-heeled, backless shoes, he decided.

"Welcome," she said throwing the door open wide.

Scottie led the way, and he followed. The many boxes had disappeared and the place was now neatly squared away.

"Have a seat. That's the only comfortable chair," she said, bustling around to turn on the air conditioner and get the things she needed to start dinner. Apparently she had already done the prep work, because she declined his offer of help—unless she thought he was too close to folding to be of much use to her.

He felt reasonably choice, though—except for the places that hurt. Many little injuries definitely made one big hurt. But his short sleep had done wonders for him. Sort of. He sat down in her one easy chair. Scottie brought out his rock collection, and Arley brought him a glass of iced tea. It was delicious, lemony and sweet, and he told her so. One of the first things he'd learned about his father's home state was that the people here had a wonderful way with iced tea.

He divided his attention between the rocks Scottie

wanted him to see and watching Arley move around the small kitchenette, aware that he would have had to have been a lot worse off not to have come to see her tonight. He admired everything about her: her concentration, hair, eyes and…breasts. He had just spent a significant number of days so occupied with things military that he could hardly think of his own name, but he had thought of her, again and again, when he least expected it. Some memory of her would suddenly arise and make him want to smile. Clearly, he was pitiful in more ways than one.

"So how's Patrick liking his job?" she asked at one point.

"Patrick who?" he asked, startled.

"Patrick, your redheaded half brother, Patrick. Let me guess. He didn't tell you?"

"No. He hasn't really had the chance. What kind of job is it?"

"Auto parts store."

"Auto parts store?"

"Well, what kind of job did you think he'd have?"

"Something on Bragg Boulevard—but not that."

She laughed. "Anyway, I had to buy a new windshield wiper and there he was. He said he was only working for the discount—so he could get some new parts he needed for his truck."

"Stranger things have happened, I guess," Will said, still trying to imagine Patrick selling car batteries and radiator hoses.

"He wanted to know if you'd been to see the house yet—where your father grew up."

Will frowned, wondering why Patrick would ask about that.

"I guess he thought I'd know—because I knew your dad was a Tar Heel," she said as if he'd asked. "So have you?" she persisted.

"No."

"Why not?"

"I...just haven't."

"He thinks you ought to go. It's empty right now. The tenants moved to Florida or something. I could go along if you need a navigator. Or some moral support."

He looked at her. She was peeling an onion. He didn't want anyone—her—to think he needed moral support.

But Arley Meehan was very perceptive. He'd realized that at the wedding reception.

"Sorry," she said, looking up from the onion. "I don't mean to meddle."

"I think it might be too far away," he said after a moment. "Farther than my travel limit."

She didn't say anything else, and Scottie brought Dot and carefully placed her in the space between Will and the arm of the chair he was sitting in. It was the prelude for Scottie himself and a book about a ladybug.

Will read it to him—several times—all the while still thinking about the Baron home place. He continued thinking about it after Scottie had taken the book and put it away and some very good smells were coming from the kitchenette. But he didn't think anything else. He closed his eyes, and that was that.

\* \* \*

Poor old paratrooper.

How could a man snore like that and still be so adorable? Arley wondered. She smiled slightly. It could be the dog pillow he was holding.

She walked quietly to the chair, stepping over his outstretched legs and coming around to the side. She and Scottie had eaten. The dishes were done. Scottie had had his bath and was already down for the night. Even he had recognized that Will Baron needed his rest, and he'd willingly donated Dot to the cause, placing the pillow carefully under Will's arm because he would "rest better." She had toyed with the idea of waking Will up so he could join them at the table, but she didn't. He was clearly exhausted, and he needed sleep more than he needed food.

She had to wake him now, though. She had to work tomorrow, and she didn't want to keep him out past his curfew. Assuming he had a curfew. She had no idea how the military worked. If he had travel limits, anything was possible. In any event, her plan had been *not* to cause him any more trouble.

She knelt by the arm of the chair. "Will," she said quietly.

Nothing.

"Will?" she said more loudly.

Still nothing.

"Will!"

He jerked awake so violently that she jumped.

"What?" he said. "What?"

"Wake up, okay?"

"I'm awake," he said, clearly trying to decide where he was. "What—sorry. I dropped off."

"Actually, it was a little more than dropping off," she said.

"How long was I asleep?"

"Oh, about…three hours."

"Three hours! Why didn't you wake me?"

"I didn't have the heart. So. I'm waking you now. I fixed up some things for you to take with you."

He looked at her blankly.

"Dinner, remember?"

"Arley, I'm sorry."

"It's okay. Don't worry about it." She smiled to show him he didn't need to be concerned. She wasn't. Her sister Kate's first personal encounter with Cal Doyle had involved his falling into a dead sleep on her couch. As far as Arley knew, *all* paratroopers did this.

Will sat for a moment, then attempted to stand, swearing softly under his breath at the pain. "Thanks for the dinner invitation," he said when he could.

"We'll do it again sometime," she said. "When you're awake."

He laughed softly. "Okay. I'll hold you to it."

"Shouldn't you see a medic or something?" she asked because of the way he was walking.

"I am a medic," he said, and then he realized she was teasing.

"Do you do this…training thing often?" she asked, just to keep him a little longer.

"Yeah," he said as he took the paper grocery bag she handed him.

"Don't tilt it," she said. She could have packed the food into recycled margarine tubs, but she used one of her best plates instead and heaped it high, knowing he'd likely feel obliged to return it.

"And the training thing is for a good reason, I guess."

He looked at her. "Yeah."

"They don't tell you anything? About when and where you'll go?"

"Not yet. I know it's coming, but that's all. Tell Scottie thanks for letting me crash on Dot."

"Thank you for salvaging her. Scott was determined to toss her out. You better go out this way so you don't scare Mrs. Bee."

They stood in front of the door that led down to the yard where he'd parked his truck.

"Can I call you sometime?" he asked. "Between injuries?"

"Do you want to?"

Neither of them answered the questions, as if to do so would open some door that they both suspected was better left closed.

They stood looking at each other, until he turned to go. She reached out and tapped the place where she'd written her phone number on the grocery bag with a permanent marker.

He looked at the number. Then he looked at her, but he wasn't sure if he ought to. He didn't quite know what to do with her, and she loved that he didn't. But the truth was that she didn't know what to do with him, either.

"Well," he said after a moment. "Good night. And thanks."

"You're welcome, Specialist." She opened the door wider and tried not to smile. "I know this is too little too late, but be careful in the dark, okay?"

He was already halfway down the steps when she said it, and he stopped and looked up at her. She could sense the smile more than see it, and she thought he was getting it finally. If she didn't keep him off balance, it wouldn't be from the lack of trying.

She stood and watched him go the rest of the way down the steps and into the yard. Then she closed the door, her mind already replaying the evening, which had consisted mostly of watching a much-too-appealing man sleep.

## Chapter Six

"I hate to complain, but aren't you supposed to at least make some kind of effort to regale me?" Patrick asked Will.

"I'm regaling," Will said. "But I have to tell you the U.S. Army is not into facilitating the entertainment of out-of-town guests—not with the pay scale or the free time. This is the best I can do."

"Tell me about it," Patrick said as he sat down in the orange booth for yet another meal of burgers and fries.

The two half brothers had managed a short jaunt around Fayetteville, mostly to get pictures of themselves at the Airborne and Special Operations museum to send to the children in the family—as soon as either of them had enough money to have copies printed.

"So have you seen Miss Arley again—awake, I mean?" Patrick asked.

"No."

"Probably not a good idea anyway."

"What do you mean?"

A small group of giggling preschoolers came into the restaurant, each grasping a loop on a long rope, that kept them together for their outing. The children, if not their teachers, were enjoying the rope immensely, snaking like a kid caterpillar up to the counter in anticipation of fast food and a toy in a box. Will couldn't keep from smiling. He couldn't keep from looking around the place to see if this happened to be the day when Arley and Scottie ate out, as well. He caught himself on the alert for them—for her—every place he went, unsuccessfully so far. He'd actually asked Kate about her, and learned that Arley had finally moved from temp work to a full-time job—some sort of teacher's aide with Head Start. She'd be good with children. He was certain of that.

He looked at Patrick across the table. "What do you mean?" he asked again.

"Okay, since you asked. She's dug in here and she's got baggage. You don't want to get tangled up with a woman like that."

"Patrick, what do you know about women like Arley?"

"I know a lot more than you do, bro. *You* are that kind of woman's worst nightmare—a man just passing through. You belong to the United States Army and to the Navajo Nation, and you've got no intention of hanging around. You couldn't, even if you wanted to.

Besides, somebody like her isn't ever going to understand somebody like you."

"Maybe I'm not looking for understanding."

"Right. Just take what you want and move on, especially when there's a little kid in the picture. That's you, all over. You know I'm not into telling people how to run their lives. If you want to go set your hair on fire, ordinarily I'd say have at it and don't expect me to call the fire department. But you're my brother, pre-train wreck. You can't blame me for wanting to point out there's something on the tracks, especially if you don't see it."

"I see it," Will said.

Patrick looked at him for a moment. "Yeah, maybe you do. Hence the perpetually cheerful countenance of late. I don't know. Maybe you ought to just go for it and get it out of your system."

"Yeah, that always works," Will said because he'd been watching Patrick trying to get something out of his system for as long as he could remember. Or maybe it was simply that Patrick, unlike Will and Meggie, had acquired all of their father's wayward genes.

"So are you going to go see Baron manor?" Patrick asked, changing the subject.

Will didn't say anything, wondering why Patrick was so hell-bent for him to go there. He could feel Patrick waiting.

"I don't need to," he said finally. "It's just a house."

"It's where the old man grew up, bro. You've been trying to figure him out since you were three. Seeing the house might make him real for you."

"He's real enough."

"He's real enough for me—*I* can remember him. Or I can remember him always leaving, dumping Meggie and me on Sloan and just disappearing. All three of us lucked out there. She stepped up to the plate for the kids he didn't want when neither one of our real mothers would do it."

Will looked at him. Sometimes he forgot that Patrick and Meggie's mother hadn't been in the picture any more than Margaret Madman had.

"Here," Patrick said, taking a folded sheet of paper out of his hip pocket. "This is the boonie route to the house. In case you change your mind. Look. I…just don't want you to have any regrets about…anything. The place might burn down or they might want to put a highway through the living room."

Or Will might go marching off to the sandbox and not come back again.

Patrick grinned suddenly.

"What?" Will asked.

"Nothing. I was just thinking about you and Arley. All that choice loveliness—and you snoring on the couch."

"I wasn't on the couch."

"Oh, great. Sprawled and drooling in a chair, were you?" Patrick said, punching him on the arm, and they both laughed, the advice session over.

After Will had said goodbye to Patrick, accepting the directions to the Baron house and some money Patrick insisted he take, he intended to go back to the barracks but he didn't. Inspired by his new unexpected cash, he turned right instead of left at a crucial intersection and headed toward Mrs. Bee's house. He had Arley's dinner plate wrapped in newspaper on the front seat. He had intended to give it to Kate to return to Arley, but now was as good a time as any to do it himself.

He parked on the street, unwrapped the plate and got out, crossing the yard and heading around to the back porch. Scottie was sitting on the top step with his backpack beside him.

"Hey, Scottie," Will said. "Where's your mom?"

"Upstairs talking to my dad. Are you going to sleep here some more?" he asked, and Will laughed.

"Not today—"

He stopped because Scott McGowan suddenly pushed open the screen door. His eyes went immediately to the plate Will was holding.

"How is it you're in the military and you've got so much free time?" he asked. He was smiling.

But Will knew a challenge when he heard it, and he had to reach deep not to react to the deliberate cage-rattling. Getting in the crosshairs for unapproved fraternizing with a civilian's ex-wife was one thing. Getting there for pitching that civilian headfirst off a little old lady's back porch was something else again. "Yeah, army life is rough—but somebody's got to do it."

They stared at each other. Scott McGowan blinked first.

"Let's go, Scottie," he said abruptly to his son, snatching up the backpack and pulling on the back of the boy's shirt.

"'Bye, Will," Scottie said.

"'Bye, buddy," Will said. He wondered where Dot was—hidden in the backpack or left behind in case Scott wanted to toss her in the trash again.

The screen door squeaked opened, and Arley came onto the porch. She looked...miserable.

"Hey," Will said. "I brought your plate back."

"Oh. Thanks," Arley said. She was looking at Scott McGowan's car drive away with her son in it. Will thought she was going to cry.

She gave a quiet sigh and sat down on the top step where Scottie had been. "I keep doing it wrong," she said. "I know how much a boy needs to respect his father—both his parents—and then I hear myself saying things—" She stopped and shook her head. "I worry about Scottie all the time."

"He'll be all right," Will said, sitting down beside her, still holding the plate.

She looked at him. "Will he?"

"Yeah. He's got people around him who love him. He knows he's not going to be alone—that's the main thing."

She started to say something more, then didn't. They sat for a time without talking. A breeze rustled the big trees at the edge of the yard, the shadows moved around the corner of the porch. Will heard birds singing, but he wasn't quite sure what kind. He had been here for months and he still had a lot to learn about the place where his father had been born.

"It was good," he said for something to say. "The Tar Heel cuisine."

She smiled. "I still think you didn't know what half of it was."

"Sure I did. Fried okra, green beans with white corn, squash casserole, sugar-cured ham, mayonnaise slaw with a little red pepper ground in it—and peach custard pie."

"Gwen made the pie," she said. "She's the only one of us who can make pies like our mom."

"Gwen should open a bake shop."

"I would tell her you said that, but she might decide to do it. And she'd either burn the place down or blow the place up."

"Accident-prone, is she?"

"We all marvel that she's still here."

The conversation faded again. He was still holding the plate.

"I need a navigator," he said without prelude—because his military training had made him decisive when the situation called for it, and he saw no point in being coy.

"A navigator?" she asked, apparently not remembering her earlier offer.

"I've got some free time and I was thinking of making a two-hour trip in an hour and a half."

"You're going to go see your father's house?"

"That's the plan. Patrick gave me the directions. I was thinking maybe I'd go and take some pictures," he said, deciding on the particulars of the venture on the spot. *See the hill, take the hill.* "For Sloan. My aunt. She hasn't been there in a long time. You want to come along? Moral support?"

She hesitated. "This is sort of a…personal journey for you. I'm not sure you'll want anybody tagging along."

"Not 'anybody,' no. Just you."

"Why?"

"So I don't get lost," he said, deliberately avoiding the question he thought she was really asking.

She smiled again. "Okay. When?"

"Right now, if you can," he said because he was pressed for time to get this impromptu mission done.

"Okay," she said again, but he could see her trying to shore up her emotions from the latest encounter with her ex-husband.

"Okay, then," he said.

"Let me put the plate away and leave Mrs. Bee a note. She worries."

He waited until Arley came back outside with her purse and her cell phone. They walked together toward the truck—until she suddenly stopped.

"It runs," he said. "Really."

"No. The truck is fine—reminds me of my dad's, only yours is better. His had grass growing in the floorboard. Are you sure you want me to come along?" she asked again.

"I'm sure, why?"

"I know you got…lit," she said. "Because you talked to me at the reception."

"Lit up," he said. "It wasn't that bad. It was a strong suggestion that came from misinformation."

"I don't want to cause you any trouble."

"You said you aren't looking to patch things up with Scott. That's good enough for me. It's going to have to be good enough for the army. Scott, too."

"Scott has a way of causing people problems."

"Arley, I don't want to cause you any trouble, either."

She smiled suddenly. "We're starting to sound like those chipmunks in the Disney cartoons. I'm glad you want a navigator—and Scott is going to think whatever he wants to think, no matter what I do. So let's go."

She waved to a neighbor, an elderly man watering his potted flowers across the street. The neighbor waved back.

"Mrs. Bee's aspiring boyfriend," she said. "She says he just wants somebody to wait on him hand and foot like his first wife did. He doesn't hang around as much since Scottie and I moved in."

"That's a good thing, I guess."

"Very good, Mrs. Bee says. Dot got her bandages off, by the way," she said as she got into the truck. "She's beginning to look a little like Frankenstein," she said when he got in on his side.

"Nah. It gives her character."

He checked to make sure the camera was in the glove compartment, then started the truck and gave her Patrick's sheet of paper with the directions, quite a lot of them as it turned out. The radio was set to 96.5 FM, the "golden oldie" station because it was the only one that would come in with any kind of certainty on the truck radio.

"Off or on?" he asked her. "It's the only thing I can get."

"On," she said, and they started on their way with Diana Ross and the Supremes singing in the background.

He drove down Bragg Boulevard and he kept glancing in Arley's direction, amazed at how comfortable he felt with her and how unsettled. He wanted to attribute his turmoil to his decision to go digging around his family tree, but it wasn't just that and he knew it. It was Arley Meehan, formerly McGowan. She was so pretty, dressed in an attention-getting but not-too-short pink skirt and a little T-shirt with a sequined scene of Paris on it. She was still sad and worrying about Scottie. Maybe he could work on that.

"How's Patrick?" she asked as they rode toward the secondary highway Patrick had indicated.

"He's…concerned about train wrecks," Will said truthfully.

"Well, as long as he isn't one. How's he doing selling car parts?"

"Great, I imagine. Patrick can sell things other people couldn't give away."

They reached the third intersection in the directions.

"That way," she said, pointing to the left.

He turned, and they headed out of town in a direction he'd never been before—in more ways than one.

His brother hadn't been kidding about the "boonie" route. It was already apparent that the trip was going to involve only secondary roads. In a short time, Will and Arley were traveling down a narrow highway with only the sandy shoulder and a ditch between the pavement and a long, thick stand of trees growing on both sides. There were a lot of hardwoods as well as the ever-present pines, but these were not the tall kind that lined the Fort Bragg section of Bragg Boulevard. Will still missed the wide-open spaces of the desert and it was like driving down a green leafy hallway.

The trees gave way to open farmland—fields of tobacco, he thought, and then corn. The corn grew tall and crowded, lush and green, nothing like the corn hills some of the traditional Navajo still planted at home.

*Plant when the moon is new, harvest when it's full.*

A memory rose in his mind, one of walking among the circular hills of blue corn with one of the old Navajo men, trying to learn the importance of the corn pollen and its symbolic connection to the healing ceremonies and to life itself. It seemed so long ago.

He kept glancing at the passing scenery, the places where people lived. Houses with porches and green grassy yards. Trailers, alone and in clusters. Random cottage businesses—a beauty shop, a lawn mower blade and chain saw sharpener, a fabric and remnant outlet setup in a garage. He wondered how much the area had changed from the time when his father had lived here. Maybe his father wouldn't even recognize it.

There was one constant—the greenness of the land, once again making Will understand what Sloan had given up to marry Lucas Singer and stay in Window Rock to help raise her brother's half-Navajo child.

"Were you kidding about your four mothers?" Arley said as they rode along.

"No."

"Tell me about them."

"It's complicated."

"Tell me anyway. Sloan raised you, you said. And your birth mother…"

"Kidnapped me when I was three," he said with a candor that surprised her.

"Are you serious?"

"Unfortunately."

"She gave you back, though."

"Not exactly. Patrick took matters into his own hands. He was about sixteen or so. He and another boy found where she was hiding me and stole me back again."

"Then what happened?"

"Custody trials mostly. Margaret Madman—she's my birth mother—lost custody to the tribe. Sloan did, too." He didn't tell her about how Patrick's rebellious teenage behavior had contributed a great deal to the decision. "But Sloan didn't give up. She and the tribe compromised. Lillian—that's the kick-butt lawyer—helped bring it about. Sloan married Lucas and stayed in Window Rock to raise me."

"Do you ever see her? Margaret Madman?"

"No. I tried to get her attention for a while when I was younger. She wasn't interested." He didn't say anything else for a time, his mind on the woman whose alcohol consumption had taken away her interest in everything.

"What about your other mothers?"

"That would be my half sister Meggie and Lucas's mother, Dolly. Dolly was running the receiving home where they took me after my dad got hurt, where I stayed after he died. I couldn't get anything past either one of them."

"Lucas…your stepfather-uncle by marriage."

"Right," he said, more than a little pleased that she remembered.

"Tell me about your last girlfriend," Arley said, apparently to ambush him. But, for once, her question didn't catch him off guard.

"She's married and has three children," he said without hesitation.

"Broke your heart, did she?"

"Pretty much. My fault, though. I wanted her to stand in one place and wait until I got around to her. It wasn't a good plan."

"So how's your heart now?"

"It's fine."

"So why didn't you call me?"

"Scared to," he said. He was teasing, but also telling the truth: his not calling had nothing to do with the army's opinion of their relationship. When he glanced at her, she was grinning ear to ear. "What?"

"You never say what I expect you to say, Baron."

"Neither do you," he said.

"What is that?" she asked, noticing the tattoo on his forearm.

"Tribal band."

"That's not a band, Specialist. That's a patch."

"The army frowns on bands."

"Ah. I'm familiar with that concept—army disapproval."

"It's amazing what seems like a good idea when you've been club-hopping all night."

"You club-hop?"

"I've been known to."

"So…is it Navajo?"

"No. It's kids-your-mama-wouldn't-let-you-play-with Airborne, if anything—band of brothers—only there are three sisters in the band. We all got one. I'm not sure where the women had theirs put, though—what?" he asked because of the expression on her face.

"It's nice," she said. "That kind of bend-the-rule bonding." She looked at Patrick's directions again. "I hope we can do this in the opposite direction," she said as they made yet another turn.

"No problem," he said. "I'll remember."

She looked at him. "That's what you do, right? Remember?"

"Yeah. It's why I can—"

"What?" she asked when he didn't continue. "What were you going to say?"

"It's why I can—could—be a *hataalii*. You have to have a good memory for detail for the sand paintings and the chants. They don't work if you leave anything out. I'll remember the landmarks."

The truck had no working air conditioner, and the "coolness" depended entirely on how fast Will drove and if the windows were open. If Arley minded roughing it, if she was having second thoughts, it didn't show. Her hair blew in the wind and she had kicked off her shoes. She watched the passing scenery, clearly more relaxed than she'd been earlier.

"Don't you have any questions?" she asked at one point.

"About…?"

"The Tar Heel flora and the fauna."

"None at this time," he said.

"So how homesick are you?" she asked without looking at him.

"Didn't we cover that?"

"I mean right now."

"Now, I'm not homesick at all."

"Just a little worried about your brother," she suggested, her ability to see what he thought was hidden apparently still intact.

"Patrick does his own thing," he said to sum up his brother in one sentence.

She looked at him—as if she were considering what he'd just said. But she didn't say anything. After a moment, she went back to looking at trees, houses and the occasional car. He was comfortable with the silence. Waiting until the other person felt ready to speak was a Navajo indicator of having been "raised."

"I do have one question," he said after a time. "How's the Head Start job?"

"The salary's not great, but it's better than what I was getting doing temp work. The hours are really good. Now all I have to worry about is making ends meet and cuts in federal funding."

"Me, too," he said, making her smile.

He didn't need to talk anymore and neither did she. He appreciated her proximity instead. And in the background the Four Tops were getting ready for the heartache to come.

I even like the way he drives, Arley thought. How could she like the way a man drove a truck? How could she like the way he slept? He *snored,* for heaven's sake. She sighed and checked for any emotions that might suggest a certain need to rethink her decision to come along on this trip. There were none. She wasn't having second thoughts. She was glad he had asked her to go, and even more glad that she'd accepted.

*It's because he's kind to Scottie.*

She always came back to that and she decided that was the reason she felt so…content. It had nothing to do with his smiling yet sad eyes or his strength. He had a certain gentleness, in spite of his rocky childhood. Or maybe because of it. But he hadn't been intimidated in the least by Scott's posturing at the wedding reception or during their most recent encounter on Mrs. Bee's back porch. Scott clearly hadn't liked finding Will Baron on the premises—again. He especially hadn't liked that Will had been holding one of her best dinner plates or that Scottie called him by his first name. But, for once, Scott had kept his confrontational tendencies in check. She had no problem imagining Will tending to the wounded or wielding a high-powered weapon if he needed to, and she thought maybe Scott didn't, either.

But the real problem was the way she was feeling right now.

Comfortable.

Not worried.

Weak in the knees from pure animal attraction.

That last item wasn't good. It wasn't good at all. She had firmly established that she enjoyed talking to Will, perturbing him, ruffling his…harmony, but she was also feeling the very things Grace had suspected she might be feeling from the outset. Whether or not she'd been attracted to him initially wasn't the question. It was, and

always had been, a matter of degree, which was unde-
niably significant at the moment. The question was
whether or not Grace had been mistaken about Arley's
motivation.

Yes. She was.

Arley was *not* trying to make her ex-husband jealous,
regardless of how "Arley-like" that might have once
been. She had moved on from the McGowan phase of
her life; her only link now was the little boy whose
leaving had pained her so earlier. Now, with Will, she
was opening a door to a corridor with no idea whatsoever where it would lead.

"Which way?" Will asked because there were signs
indicating that they were approaching a crossroads.

She reached for the sheet of paper again. "Left," she
said and pointed in that direction. She thought.

Will looked at her. "Would that be left left or right
left?"

"It would be the way I point, not what I say."

"Got it," he said, trying not to grin.

"Okay," Arley said. "I probably should have told you
I don't know which is which—since I'm navigating."

"Probably," he said. "No problem, though, as long
as your fingers work."

"My thoughts exactly."

"Which left was that again?"

"That one," she said, pointing to show him.

"How are you with up and down?"

"That I know—and quit making fun of me."

"I'll try," he said.

They rode for a time in silence, but she could still feel

his amusement. She hadn't been trying to be "airhead" cute. She really was side-to-side directionally challenged.

There was a small convenience store just beyond the crossroads, and they pulled in. Arley got out to look at the fresh produce while Will put gas in the truck.

"How's it going?" the old man who was selling corn and tomatoes and watermelon asked Will when he joined her. "The army treating you good?"

"Sir?" Will said.

"The haircut, son. If you ain't at Bragg, I'm a monkey's uncle."

"I'm at Bragg, sir," Will admitted.

"You been over there yet?" the old man asked, apparently referring to the recent deployments.

"Not yet, sir."

"You two married?"

"No, sir."

"Well, then, you got a tough decision to make. I got married before I went overseas—made it easier for both of us. But I reckon it's hard to know if you ought to or not—if it's going to help you or worry you to death. Anything else you want, honey?" he said to Arley.

"That's all," she said, giving the six ears of corn she'd selected. He put them into a plastic recycled grocery bag, mischievously adding an extra ear as a bonus when she handed him her money.

"This is good eatin' corn," he promised her, and she smiled. Scottie loved corn on the cob, and these she could afford. She'd fix them when he got back from his weekend with Scott—a surprise for their Sunday night supper.

## *Chapter Seven*

Will recognized the Baron home place immediately because of the sunroom annex on one end of the house and because of the photograph Sloan had once given him. He slowed the truck, but he didn't decide until the last moment to turn in. The driveway was dirt and gravel and deeply rutted. Arley had to hold on to the door until the truck bounced to a stop under the shade trees.

Hands resting on the steering wheel, he stared at the house through the windshield. It was so strange, finally seeing it. He'd always known, intellectually, at least, that it was an actual place, but being here made it different somehow. His past, the past he could never quite visualize, was suddenly real.

Real.

But no less alien. He got out of the truck. The grass needed mowing and there were tall treelike bushes blooming in the yard. They were common here, but he couldn't remember what they were called, in spite of his stellar memory for detail.

"Crepe myrtles," he said under his breath as Arley came to stand beside him. He could feel her watching him, but he said nothing. He was preoccupied with a sudden urge to groom the place. He wanted to pick up the road trash that had blown into the yard, nail down a bowed porch step, replace the numerous cracked windowpanes in the sunroom windows.

"Here comes somebody," Arley said, and he turned to see a tall middle-aged man approaching from the next house down the road. Will walked into the front yard to meet him.

"You all wanting to rent this place?" the man asked. "I've got the key if you want to see inside."

"I'm Will Baron, sir," Will said. "My family owns it. I'm just looking around."

"Baron? You kin to Sloan?"

"Mark's son, sir. But Sloan raised me."

"Oh, yeah. I remember that. A sad thing, that was. I was in school with Mark—he was a couple years ahead of me. He had more kids than just you if I'm remembering right."

"Two more—my brother and sister."

"Sloan's still in Arizona, I reckon. I always wanted to get out that way. You wanting to see the inside the house?"

"If I could, sir," Will said. "I've never been here before. I thought I'd take some pictures for Sloan."

"Well, I reckon that'll be all right—you being in the family. I'll have to ask you for some ID, though," the man said.

Will got out his wallet and removed his driver's license, waiting while the man studied it carefully.

"All right then," he said after a moment. "That's good enough for me. Ain't nothing in there to steal, anyway. The house itself is still in pretty good shape. Needs paint, of course, and some general fixing up. You should have seen it when your grandparents were alive. Mrs. Baron—Miss Addie, we always called her— she'd put up this big Christmas tree in the sunroom there. Every single year while she was living, and I mean *big*. We'd always come this way every chance we got just so we could see it. It weren't Christmas around here until she got her tree up. Well, I'll be going on about my business. Just make sure the door's shut tight when you leave. When you talk to Sloan, tell her Walt asked after her. She'll know who I am." He looked up at the sky, then in the direction over Will's shoulder. "Looks like it's going to rain. If you need gas before you head back, my son-in-law's got a place down the road yonder. You can get something to eat there, too. Oh, uh, the upstairs bathroom is working. I keep the water turned on in case people looking to rent need it."

"Thanks. Nice meeting you, sir," Will said, shaking the man's hand.

The man turned and walked up onto the porch, nodding to Arley as he passed. He unlocked the door and left in the direction he'd come.

*Your grandparents.*

How easily the man had said it. For Will, it was the concept that was so hard to grasp.

The wind was picking up. The sky was overcast, a perfectly smooth bluish gray expanse with no clouds at all. But the blueness faded into a deep gray toward the southwest. Will stood for a moment looking at it, then walked toward the house.

"You know anything about places like this?" he asked Arley, glad she was with him.

"Like what?"

"Like…what the rooms would have been used for," he said as he stepped up on the porch.

"I think I can guess," she said.

He opened the screen door and walked inside, letting her follow behind him. The hallway was cool and dark and ended in a straight shot at the back door of the house as far as he could see. He suddenly remembered something Sloan had told him about his father. When Mark Baron was a young boy, he used to play with the small whirlwinds that would pop up in the summer heat, jumping into the middle of them, chasing after them around the yard and down the drive. Once, she said, just as he opened the front screen door, one blew into the house with him, knocking pictures from the walls as it passed through the hallway and outside again through the back screen door. He remembered, too, one of the old Navajo men who heard her tell the story saying that even then Coyote had been trying to bring Mark Baron to his bad end on the reservation.

Will took a quiet breath and looked around him. The man, Walt, was right. There wasn't much to steal. Will could tell that the dark bare floors were hardwood and that the banisters on the stairway were probably hand-turned. He could see a phone jack on the baseboard in the hallway, and he wondered if this was where Sloan had taken the call from Window Rock that night when tribal policeman Lucas Singer had telephoned to tell her that her brother had been seriously injured and to ask what should be done with his three-year-old child, a child she hadn't even known existed.

"I think this was the living room," Arley said, standing at the doorway to the room on Will's left. "I like the French doors to the sunroom."

He looked at her. He had been so deep in thought and she was being so unintrusive that for a moment he'd forgotten she was with him. "Sloan said she used to sleep out there on summer nights when she was a little girl. Something about stars and lightning bugs. I think it was a 'princess-in-the-castle' kind of a thing."

"Works for me," Arley said. "That door should lead to the dining room, then the kitchen should be beyond that. The first room on the other side of the hallway was probably a front bedroom—maybe a den. It's a big house. Reminds me a little of Mrs. Bee's."

They walked through the living room into the sunroom and back out. In spite of the general need for paint and repairs, everything looked and smelled clean. Arley led the way through what she thought was the dining room and into a large airy Norman Rockwell kind of kitchen. It, too, smelled of mopped floors and bleach.

Will inspected each room with the growing realization that, while the place had become a solid reality in his mind, his father remained as elusive as ever. Will didn't *feel* anything. He couldn't sense the man's presence at all. Wherever Mark Baron's restless *chindi* might be, it wasn't here.

They walked upstairs. A new-looking oriental patterned runner ran almost the entire length of the hallway. It was padded, muffling their footsteps as they walked to look into the first room.

"Do you know which one was your father's?" Arley asked.

"No," he said. "From what people said, my guess is he'd have had the room he could get in and out of without anybody catching him."

Arley's cell phone rang and she answered it. "Hey, Scottie," she said, and Will wondered if the boy could hear her forced cheerfulness. He walked away to give her some privacy, moving down the hallway to a room at the back.

He opened the door and stepped inside. It was simply a large, high-ceilinged room without furniture, nothing masculine or feminine about it. Any essence of a Baron presence that might have remained had long since been lost in the parade of subsequent renters.

He walked to the closet and opened the door. It was too dark inside to see much. He took the small flashlight he always carried out of his jeans pocket and shined it around.

Nothing. Not even a hanger.

He looked in the corners. He was about to close the door when he saw something scratched on the wood at the back.

He stepped closer and shined the light on it to see.

*Mark Baron was here.*

There may have been a date, but he couldn't make it out.

*Patrick Baron was here* had been carved right beneath it.

There was no room for another son to document his presence.

He closed the closet door and walked out into the hallway. It was hot upstairs. Thunder rumbled in the distance. He could hear Arley still talking to Scottie on the phone.

He walked to the end of the hall and tried to raise the three-over-three window. Surprisingly, it opened easily, but the counterweights no longer worked. He found a stick on the sill and propped it open, then stood, watching the trees sway, feeling the strong breeze coming ahead of the storm.

"It's not working, is it?" Arley said at his elbow.

"What?" he asked, trying to keep his tone light and making every effort not to look at her.

"This trip. You aren't connecting with him."

"No," he said after a moment. And it was true. If he had dared hope that he might finally achieve some sense of belonging, of knowing who he was, by coming here, he was mistaken.

"I'm sorry."

"Probably for the best. Less confusion in the long run."

"You want to look around some more?" she asked just as drops of rain began to pelt the windowpane.

The sound of the rain grew louder overhead, and there was a loud crack of thunder.

"Male rain," he said, watching the trees bend under the onslaught of the rising storm.

"Rain has a gender?"

"Where I come from, it does."

"What's a female rain like?"

"Steady. Gentle. Soft."

He finally looked at her. He didn't say anything and neither did she. After a moment, she stepped closer.

"I know you're tough—go, Airborne, and all that—and I don't want you to panic because this is not because I think you need it," she said. "This is because I need it—so *I'll* feel better."

With that, she slid her arms around him, resting her head against his shoulder. "I'm sorry," she whispered again. "You've come a long way to find him."

He returned the embrace, holding her tightly, allowing himself to take the comfort she was offering. Just this once, he would acknowledge his long-held desire for someone to understand. He could do that safely enough; he wasn't embarrassed by it. The emptiness he was feeling was nothing new, nothing he couldn't handle, and her reaching out to him didn't really mean anything—to either of them.

He took a deep breath. He intended to end the embrace, to step away while he still could, but she lifted her head and looked at him. She was so close, her body soft and warm against his. The compassion he saw in her eyes made him stay. He tried to smile and didn't quite make it. Instead, he slowly lowered his mouth to lightly touch hers.

And he was lost. Suddenly nothing mattered but being with her, as close as he could get. He was starving, and she was what he wanted. His mouth sought hers, and she returned his kiss. He lifted her up off the floor just to have her closer.

*More.*

That was the only thought in his mind. That was all he wanted.

*More.*

She leaned back to look into his eyes again.

"Right here," she said.

And then they were both kneeling, both lying down on the carpet runner in the upstairs hallway.

"Arley…" he started to say.

She cupped his face in her hands. "Right here," she said again, pressing against him so he would know.

His hands moved over her body, his touch urgent and full of purpose. He raised up to remove his T-shirt, then helped remove hers, some part of his mind briefly noting that there were fragile sequins on it. But the rest of his mind was dedicated to only one objective.

To have her.

Right here.

They didn't talk; there was nothing to say. There was only the need. His. Hers.

There was no time for talking, for thinking. Clothing had to be removed. Bodies had to slide together, to touch, to taste.

The rain beat on the roof and blew in through the open window. He was inside her, lost in the pleasure of it. At the end, he said her name.

The cell phone was ringing. Arley opened her eyes and removed herself from Will's embrace to fumble for it in her purse. She held on to his hand for a moment, caressing it once before she gave her attention to the persistent alert from the cell.

"Hello?"

"Arley, is that you?" someone said—she thought.

The sound kept breaking up.

"Hello?" she said again.

"Arley," the voice said again. "Are you still with Will Baron?"

She glanced in Will's direction. "Mrs. Bee?"

"Fort Bragg is looking for him, Arley," Mrs. Bee said. "Do you know where he is?"

"Yes," Arley said. "He's right here. Do you want to talk to him?"

"Oh, no. You can tell him. A soldier called here looking for him. He wouldn't leave a message. I was afraid it might be important. Oh, dear. I didn't write down his name. I was sure I'd remember, but—"

She could hear Mrs. Bee sigh.

"I think it had something to do with a singing cowboy."

"You mean like…Roy something?"

"Roy Rogers? No, not him. Oh, dear. If I remember I'll call back."

"Okay, Mrs. Bee. Anything else?"

"No. No, that's all," Mrs. Bee said. "It's all right that I called your cell phone, isn't it?"

"Of course, Mrs. Bee. Thanks. Fort Bragg wants you," Arley said to Will as she ended the call. "I think. Mrs. Bee said whoever called had something to do with a singing cowboy."

He frowned. She could sense him trying to return to

the place they'd been *before* they'd made wild abandoned love on a carpet runner. He began putting his clothes on, his face closed and unreadable.

"Aren't you worried about why?" she asked.

"Why isn't the bottom line in the army," he said. "Ever."

She sat for a moment and then began picking up her discarded clothing. She kept glancing at him as she dressed, still trying to read his face—what little emotion there was on it.

"You're very…quiet," she said.

"Yeah." He was sitting on the floor beside her and she reached to touch the strong, muscular expanse of his back.

"What are you doing?" she asked, and she didn't mean zipping up his jeans.

"Waiting."

"For what?"

"For you to regret this."

"I don't regret it."

"Not yet," he said.

She didn't say that it was her usual policy not to worry about consequences until there were some. She moved so he would have to look at her. "I don't regret it," she said again. "Why would I? We're both adults. We like each other. I like you, anyway. Especially since all the cuts and bruises have healed."

He smiled suddenly, and she returned it, wrapping her arms around him, giving him a brief hug.

"I guess we have to get going, don't we? ASAP—or whatever it is you soldiers say."

"Faster than that," he said, getting to his feet and pulling her up with him.

"Will—?"

"What?" he said.

She kept watching his face. *She* was worried about the Fort Bragg call if he wasn't, and it occurred to her suddenly that she needed to take her cue from him. "Nothing," she said. "Let's go."

It was still raining when he locked the front door of the Baron house and made certain it was secure. They both got drenched running to the truck.

"We didn't take any pictures," she said suddenly as he backed out onto the road. She wasn't trying to make him laugh, but he did.

"No. Not one." He reached for her hand, and she slid her fingers between his.

She didn't say anything else. He didn't want to talk, she knew that. She simply sat there, holding his hand.

And making comparisons.

She had enjoyed the physical side of her marriage. She was even willing to concede—now—that physical attraction may have been all there was to it. But Will Baron was nothing like Scott. Nothing. And she was already searching to find a way to be with him again. He still made her knees weak. She wanted to feel his hands on her, to make love with him—in a bed—and not have him need to leave.

She gave a quiet sigh, and he squeezed her hand. She smiled at him, wondering if he realized what a shameless woman he'd fallen in with.

## Chapter Eight

"Where the hell have you been?"

Will had made it all the way to his door without incident or inquiry. In fact, nothing out of the ordinary seemed to be going on at all, at least nothing that required his attention. He had actually begun to consider the possibility that Mrs. Bee had been mistaken about the call from a Fort Bragg singing cowboy.

But, unfortunately, Will suddenly recognized the significance of the name, and here he was now. "Cowboy" Copus, clearly distressed.

"That would be your business, how?" Will said as he unlocked his door. He had no intention of stopping to chat. He had too much to think about, some of it pleasant.

Beyond pleasant.

The rest had to do with knowing exactly where he was heading with Arley Meehan and being determined to go as far as possible anyway.

"Yeah, well, there's a lot of things around here that ain't none of my business, son, but you don't see me walking off when one of my buddies needs me, even if he don't know it."

"What are you talking about?"

"I'm talking about that big redheaded relative of yours—the one with the attitude."

"What attitude?" he asked because he had no doubt whatsoever about the identity of the relative.

"The attitude that made him try to get on post when he was too drunk to walk, much less drive. You wouldn't believe the BAC he blew."

"Ah, damn it! Where is he?"

"After considerable persuasion from yours truly, they let me and Trask take his sorry ass back to the motel, that's where he is. After we stopped at the pawn shop so he could hock his watch and the turquoise stuff to get enough money to pay for another night, of course."

"Did he say anything?"

"Not much. He was in the early blue phase where they don't talk. You know—just before they start muttering and bawling."

"I'd better go check on him—"

"No-o-o-o," Copus assured him. "The sergeant saw you come in. There ain't no going anywhere for you, or me, or anybody else they can eyeball. All off-duty downtime is hereby cancelled and we whose pleasure it is to serve get to stand by for some good old unscheduled, spur-of-the-moment army chores. You better saddle up."

"Where have you been?"

Arley sighed and gave her sister her full attention. "Why don't you just say what you mean, like you usually do, Grace? You don't want to know *where*. You want to know *with whom*."

"All right. Let's cut to the chase, then. Did you go off somewhere with that paratrooper?"

"I did, yes. And I came back with a marriage proposal."

"Arley! Are you crazy? What is Scott going to say?"

"What can he say, Grace? Well, he might have some misgivings about the age difference."

"Age difference?" Grace repeated.

"Yeah. The aspiring groom must be in his eighties."

"What are you talking about?"

"The little old man selling fresh corn at a convenience store. See?" she said holding up an ear. "He said he'd marry me if Will didn't."

"Oh, very cute, Arley."

"Maybe I'll give him to Mrs. Bee. She might like him," Arley said absently as she stuffed the corn into the her apartment-sized refrigerator. "What do you think?"

"I *think* you're asking for trouble. Scott is going to find out you're seeing that soldier—"

"Scott and Will ran into each other on Mrs. Bee's back porch this afternoon. Will had one of my dinner plates in his hand. As oblivious as my former husband can be about things, I expect he noticed the man *and* the plate. So you're worrying about a done deal here, Grace."

For once Grace didn't say anything, and that was unsettling in itself.

"I like him, Grace," she said after a long moment, surprised by the quiver in her voice. "I like him a lot."

"Well—oh, for heaven's sake, don't *cry.* It'll be all right. I guess."

"Make up your mind! It can't be all right *and* the end of the world!" Arley reached for a tissue and blew her nose. "He said he'd call me—but he said he might not be able to for a while, and I…" She ended the statement with a forlorn little hand gesture that made her look as pitiful as she felt.

"You sound like you did when you were in high school and you had a crush on some dim-witted football player," Grace said.

"I know," Arley said, tearing up again. "It's crazy. I *feel* like I did when I was in high school. I want to see him again. He's so…so…"

"Not Scott McGowan," Grace finished for her.

"Exactly."

"Arley, I just hope you're not going to do anything risky with him. I'm not blind. I can see why he'd be appealing. He's got that…warrior-going-into-harm's-way thing going on for him, and some women find that totally irresistible."

Arley didn't say anything.

"Oh, great!" Grace said, throwing up her hands. "You've already done it, haven't you? Arley!"

Arley still didn't say anything. She could have said that

she'd planned ahead, that she'd been so certain of where things were heading that she hadn't left the house without birth control. But she didn't, knowing pre-planning in this case was as likely to set Grace off as irresponsibility.

Her cell phone rang—thankfully.

"Hey," the now-familiar voice said when she answered it.

"Hey," she said, smiling. She glanced at Grace in time to see her roll her eyes. Arley walked toward the double window, and turned her back on her sister.

"I can't talk long," Will said. "You haven't seen Patrick, have you?"

"No, why?"

"He's…I don't know where he is. He tried to come on post drunk. Some of the guys took him back to his motel. I'm stuck here and when I called the motel, they said he checked out. I don't know what's going on with him—I just saw him at lunchtime and he seemed pretty okay then. If you happen to see him…"

"I'll call you."

"Call the barracks. You'll probably have to leave a message. Hopefully Trask won't be taking messages and I can read it."

"Okay. Maybe I should get Grace to pound some sense into Brother Patrick. She's good at that kind of thing."

"Oh, really?" Grace said in the background. "It never seems to work on *you*."

Will heard her and laughed. "Can't hurt," he said. "I think the family's tried everything else. Arley?"

"What?"

"I'm…I can't stop thinking about you," he said,

lowering his voice as if he didn't want anyone close by to hear him.

She smiled again.

"Did you hear me?" he said, his voice still low.

"I heard you. I might be thinking about you, too."

"Might?"

"That's what I said, Specialist. I have to play a little hard to get, you know."

He laughed again, and somebody who sounded very unhappy bellowed in the background.

"Gotta go!" he said and hung up.

Arley stood for a moment holding the phone.

"Trouble in paradise?" Grace asked.

"Something's going on with Will's brother," Arley said.

"Like what?"

Arley told her what Will had told her. Grace didn't say anything.

Encouraged by Grace's conspicuous lack of acerbic comment, Arley decided to elaborate. "I think Will is really worried about him."

"Well, where could Patrick go—if he's that drunk?"

"I don't know. Some place rampant with iniquity, probably."

"Some place on Bragg Boulevard?"

"I don't know," Arley said again. "I think I'm going to ride around and see if I can see his truck anywhere."

Someone knocked at the hallway door and Arley went to answer it. Gwen stood on the threshold, and Arley was beginning to get the picture here. Two-thirds of her sisters were about to do what they did best—gang up on her.

"She's taken a lover," Grace said without prelude.

"Oh," Gwen said mildly. "Anybody we know?"

"That paratrooper. What *is* it with you people and paratroopers!"

"Please don't yell at me, Grace," Gwen said. "I *don't* have one."

"Yet," Grace said. "I just don't know what we're going to do with her."

"Well, how serious is she?"

"Hold it!" Arley yelled into the discussion. "Could you two maybe notice I'm standing right here?"

They both looked at her.

Gwen suddenly grinned. "So how was it?" she asked, raising and lowering her eyebrows once for effect.

"Gwen!" Grace said. "We're not here to get the sordid details of her love life."

"All evidence to the contrary," Arley said. "As truly wonderful as this is, I'm going to go look for Will's brother."

"Why?" Gwen asked.

"He's drunk," Grace said. "And missing, apparently."

"Oh. Well, you can't go looking for somebody drunk by yourself," Gwen said. "We'll go with you."

"No, *we* won't," Grace said. "I've got better things to do than chase down some drunk."

"Yes, we will, Grace! If we're going to look out for our Arley like we promised Mom, we can't just do it when it's convenient."

Arley and Grace both looked at this new assertive entity who had apparently taken over their sister's body.

"We can take Mrs. Bee's car," Gwen continued. "I

saw her when I came in, and she said it was time for somebody to air out 'Thelma and Louise.'"

Arley sighed. She loved Mrs. Bee's vintage Thunderbird. Mr. Bee had given it to her brand-new and, somewhere along the line, it had been named for the movie in which a similar one had a significant role. Arley just didn't love the idea of going on a possible search and rescue mission with these two sisters in it.

Gwen was already throwing open the hallway door. "Mrs. Bee! We'll take 'Thelma and Louise' out for you!"

"All right, dear," Mrs. Bee called. "I've got the keys right here."

"We've got to go look for a drunk!" Gwen called.

"Shhhhhh!" Arley and Grace hissed in unison.

"What?" Gwen said in response.

"Gwen, there are some things better left unsaid," Grace said. "Maybe Mrs. Bee doesn't want her car going where we're apparently going. Everybody in the whole congregation would probably see it."

"Oh. Now you tell me. Mrs. Bee!" she yelled out the door again.

"Yes, dear," Mrs. Bee said from a foot away, making Gwen jump. "What drunk are you looking for?"

"You scared me, Mrs. Bee," Gwen said, still clutching her chest. "What drunk are we looking for?" she repeated, glancing at both sisters for clues as to how she should proceed.

"It's Patrick," Arley said.

"Will's brother Patrick?"

"Yes. He tried to get on post when he was drinking

and now Will can't find him. He can't go look for him and he's worried about him."

"Well, I don't blame him. Any ideas where he might be?"

"None. I thought I'd ride around and see if I could see his truck."

"Good idea. I'll come, too."

"Oh—well—Mrs. Bee. We might actually find him, you know, and I don't think you'd want to—"

"Arley, honey, I don't talk about it much, but my brother Jimmy had a terrible drinking habit. It was bad before he was in the war and it was worse after. I've forgotten more about trying to get a drunken man out of harm's way than you'll ever know. I'll go call Lula Mae. She used to help me with Jimmy."

With that, Mrs. Bee left and went back downstairs.

"Now see what you've done?" Grace said to Gwen.

It didn't take long to get the reconnaissance party mobilized. In no time at all Arley was sitting in the front seat with Grace, who insisted on driving, while Gwen and Mrs. Bee settled themselves in the back. Mrs. Bee's friend, Lula Mae, notorious for her minimal bladder capacity, opted to stay behind to man the telephone in case they needed reinforcements to drag Patrick Baron out of temptation's grasp.

"Put the top down," Gwen said.

Grace gave her a look and the top stayed up. "You can recognize Patrick's truck, right?" she said to Arley as she pulled onto Bragg Boulevard.

Arley frowned. "I'm…not sure."

"What do you mean, you're not sure?"

"You saw it, too, Grace. Between the two of us, surely we can pick it out."

"I wasn't looking at his truck," Grace said, making Gwen and Arley both snicker.

"What were you looking at, Grace?" Gwen wanted to know.

"I was too aggravated with that one," she said, nodding in Arley's direction, "to notice anything."

"Too bad," Arley said. "He thinks you're cute."

"What?"

"You heard me. Patrick thinks you're cute. That's what he said, anyway. He said you all but frisked him—"

"I did not!"

"All but frisked him," Arley repeated. "Then he said you were cute—but not to tell you he said that until after he'd left."

Grace made a noise, one of her many indicators of disapproval.

Arley reached and tuned in the radio to 96.5 FM.

"Since when do you like golden-oldie music?" Grace asked.

*Since it started to remind me of making love with Will Baron on a carpet runner in the middle of a thunderstorm,* Arley thought.

"Just recently," she said.

"Oh, look," Gwen cried from the backseat as they approached one of the clubs. "Ladies' night—let's go there."

"Gwen, Patrick is not going to be hanging out at a 'ladies' night.' You see what you've done?" Grace said to Arley.

"Yes," Arley said, sighing. It was getting dark, and

she kept her eye on the parking lots of the various establishments as they drove past, but she was thinking about Will, wondering what he was doing now.

*I keep thinking about you.*

*Me, too,* she thought. *Oh, me, too.*

"That one's got a lot of trucks," Mrs. Bee said, pointing to a place that didn't seem to have an entrance.

"Slow down, Grace!" Arley said. "Turn in there."

"It looks like a biker bar!" Grace said in protest.

"Sounds about right," Arley said. "Turn, turn!"

Grace turned, but she wasn't happy about it. There was no way they could cruise through and see all the trucks up close. Somebody was going to have to get out.

"Let me out," Arley said, and Grace parked the car near the edge of the road—out of the way, to avoid any potential dings to "Thelma and Louise's" still-pristine paint job.

Arley got out and quickly ran among the trucks. None looked like a "definite," but there was one "possible" with a New Mexico license plate.

"Close enough," she said and went back to the car. "I'm going inside."

"You can't go inside! Are you crazy!" Grace said.

"I'm just going to take a quick look, Grace, and come right back out. Patrick Baron, if he's in there, isn't going to be that hard to spot."

"We'll go with you," Mrs. Bee said. "Come on, Gwen."

"I've never been in a biker bar, have you, Mrs. Bee?" Gwen asked conversationally as they crawled out of the backseat in spite of Grace's protests.

"Actually, I've been in worse," Mrs. Bee said. "But I was much younger."

"You people are crazy," Grace said. "Every one of you." But she was getting out, too. Somebody on a motorcycle roared into the parking lot and parked close to the building. Arley watched as he got off and went in through the front door.

"So that's where it is," she said. She began walking in that direction, wondering who in the world had painted a *trompe l'oeil* to make the door blend in with the wall.

She opened it and led the way into the intermittently dark interior. The lighting seemed to be a continuous work in progress, adding to the difficulty of deciding a direction in which to go. Gwen had one of her arms and Mrs. Bee had her firmly by the back of her T-shirt. The place was full of cigarette smoke and rough-looking men. The music was earsplitting hard rock, bump-and-grind variety, and a girl with long curly blond hair, wearing not much else, pranced around a shiny brass pole.

"I hear that's very good exercise," Mrs. Bee said at her elbow.

"Oh, please," Grace said.

"No, Grace. It was on television. I saw it on *The View.*"

The four of them made it almost to the bar before somebody stopped them.

"Whoa!" the man said. He was wearing a red hide-the-receding-hairline bandanna, a sleeveless sweatshirt with raveled edges and a leather vest. "Where do you four think you're going?"

"We're looking for someone," Arley said.

"Not in here, you're not. Coming in here ain't free, darlin'."

"They're going to buy something at the bar," she said. "I'm just going to see if I can find—"

"What did I just say?"

"You just said something that's going to break my heart," Arley answered. "Please. It's important. Let me see if he's in here. I won't cause any trouble—he's not a boyfriend or anything like that. I just need to make sure he's all right."

He looked at her doubtfully.

"Please," Arley said again. "I won't bother anybody. *Please.*"

She couldn't tell if the flagrant pleading was working or not.

"Okay," he said after a long moment. "You can look. Period. The rest of you hit the bar and *buy* something."

"Thank you!" Arley said. She shooed Mrs. Bee and her sisters toward the bar.

"I'm buying," she heard Mrs. Bee say. She also heard the order—orange juice on the rocks all around.

Arley moved among the patrons, surprised when the lights briefly came up again that there were actually some women in the place. If she kept moving and timed it right, she could get a brief look at most of the patrons.

"Who you looking for, sweet cheeks?" one of the men asked as she squeezed by.

"Patrick Baron," she said. "You know him?"

"Can't say I do. What does he look like?"

"Tall, red hair."

"Does he play a guitar and sing?"

"Not that I know of."

"Is he in the military?"

"No."

"Well, I'm not busy if you can't find him."

"Thanks," Arley said, moving on before the unhappy woman on his other side took exception to their conversation.

The man ignored her and went back to watching the mostly naked blonde swing herself around the brass pole.

Arley's eyes were growing accustomed to the dimness and she glanced toward the bar. Mrs. Bee was trying to hoist her petite self up onto an empty bar stool. After a few tries, one of the closest barflies set his beer mug down, gave the elderly woman a little bow, then lifted her up and carefully placed her on the stool. Gwen was busy talking to a young man, and Grace—Arley didn't know what Grace was doing. She couldn't see her expression, but her sister's body screamed "Not Happy!"

Arley went back to looking for Patrick, moving into the darker recesses of the room where the strobe lights didn't reach.

Her cell phone suddenly rang, causing numerous protests from the clientele. Clearly, this wasn't a be-available-at-all-times kind of place.

"Hello," she said, cupping her mouth as she whispered into the phone, hoping to be heard over the din.

"Please tell me you're not in a bar," her sister Kate said.

"I'm not in a bar," Arley said dutifully—just as the dancing girl executed some bizarre move on the pole and *really* thrilled the audience.

"Where are you, then?" Kate asked.

"Okay, I'm in a bar."

"You know you have really upset the paratrooper, don't you?"

"Mine or yours?"

There was dead silence on the other end of the call, and it continued for a significant length of time.

"Mine," Kate said finally. "Arley, I want you to get out of there."

"I haven't finished looking yet—and who told you where I was, anyway?"

"Oh, we just happened to see a very conspicuously out-of-place vehicle on our way home. First, we thought Mrs. Bee's car had been stolen. Lula Mae set us straight, though. Imagine my surprise when I learned you'd taken Mrs. Bee barhopping."

"It was her idea to come along, not mine."

"Arley—!"

"Okay, okay!"

"Where is the rest of your…party?"

"At the bar."

"Mrs. Bee, too?"

"Yes," Arley said, making her way in a different direction so she could keep searching.

"Is she sober?"

"Of course, she's sober! This is Mrs. Bee we're talking about. She's drinking orange juice."

"How healthful," Kate said. She gave a heavy sigh. Arley could hear somebody talking in the background. "Okay, Cal's buddies are here. They're all going to take over the search, so you and the Wild Bunch can come back home now. The guys have more of an idea where to look for Will's brother than you do, and Cal knows what he looks like. Enough said?"

"Yeah, pretty much," Arley said.

"Good. Try to get out of there without incident, will you? I can't afford bail money for all four of you."

Arley ended the call and kept looking for Patrick in the last dark corner, finally concluding that he wasn't in the place. She made her way back to the bar in time to hear one of the barflies—who didn't look old enough to be on the premises—hitting on Gwen.

"No, really. I *like* older women," he was saying as Arley walked up. "They got so much more to offer a man—brains and…" He looked Gwen up and down. "Experience."

"Don't tell me there are women who actually fall for that line," Arley said.

"Quiet, Arley," Gwen said, smiling in a way that made Arley wonder if the orange juice had been straight after all. "Let the boy talk."

## Chapter Nine

"You're next," Patrick said.

Arley stepped up on Mrs. Bee's back porch, despite what sounded like a dire warning.

Patrick was sprawled on the swing, but she barely looked at him, in spite of the fact that he was out and about so soon after his notorious evening of barhopping and that she was more than a little curious as to where Cal and his fellow paratroopers had taken him after they had dragged him out of harm's way. Whatever he'd been doing in the interim, though, he didn't seem any the worse for it, and she gave her full attention to the reason for his remark, to one Specialist Will Baron, who was wearing his green camouflage BDUs and who was clearly less than pleased about something.

But, disgruntled or not, she was so glad to see him.

"Are you looking for me?" she asked, trying to keep the conversation neutral until she could determine what was going on.

"Yeah," he said.

"I had to stay a little late at work. Somebody put most of the blue crayons in the toilet. Our ability to demonstrate blue skies, birds and oceans is now severely limited—"

"I want to talk to you," he interrupted.

"Can I put my purse down first?" she asked lightly. It was looking more and more as if Patrick's remark really had been a warning and she just might be about to experience the "lit up" phenomenon firsthand. If she had hoped to lessen Will's degree of worry about his brother, she suspected that she was about to be seriously disappointed.

There didn't seem to be any way around whatever this might be, so she took a quiet breath and set her purse on the top step. Her back hurt from lifting small children and kneeling to tie shoes at the Head Start all day, but she made no attempt to sit down anywhere. She stood and waited.

She didn't have to wait long.

"What were you thinking?" Will demanded the very second she looked at him.

"Could you be more...specific?" she said, and Patrick grinned.

"You watch yourself," Will said to him, and Patrick managed to look innocent and a little contrite at the same time. He did it so well, Arley could only guess at the amount of practice it must have taken for him to perfect it.

"Arley, I asked you if you'd *seen* him. I didn't mean for you to go into some rough bar trying to find him, for God's sake!"

"Will, I know that," Arley said.

"Patrick is my problem, not yours. Do you have any idea how dangerous that could have been? You scared the hell out of me!"

"I'm sorry. I didn't mean to worry you. It just sort of…evolved. In my own defense, it wasn't as impulsive as it looks—well, maybe it was a little impulsive. But I didn't go *alone*."

"And that's another thing," Will said. "I get to have little Mrs. Bee on my conscience, too? Not to mention Gwen and Grace."

"Mrs. Bee was a schoolteacher for a long time. She's used to…unusual people."

"That must have come in handy, then." He looked at his watch. "I can't talk about this now. I'm on duty in twenty minutes. We are *not* done here," he said to his brother. He started to say something more to Arley— twice—then didn't. He walked off instead.

"Well, that went well," Patrick said.

Arley sat down on the step beside her purse.

"He's really mad," she said.

"As mad as I've ever seen him," Patrick said. "You got off easy. You should have heard him before you got here."

She looked at him. "This is all your fault."

"Pretty much," he said. "I miscalculated."

"Miscalculated what?"

"How far gone he is. And in that light, I've got a question for you."

"What is it?"

"Are you just playing around here or what?"

"I don't know what you mean," she said.

"Sure, you do. I want to know what your intentions are regarding my brother."

Her first impulse was to be flippant. Her second was to be offended. She went with her third—the truth.

"I like him. A lot."

"Most people do," Patrick said. "What I want to know is how bad are you for him? Are you using him to get at your ex, or is this what you do for fun—take on some unsuspecting good guy like he is, grind him up and then move on?"

"No," she said evenly. "It's not. And I don't think I want to have this conversation." She got to her feet and turned to go.

"You don't know anything about him," Patrick said.

"I know he was a *hataalii*. I know about Meggie and Sloan and Dolly. And *you*. I know about Margaret Madman. I know she kidnapped him and you saved him. And I know how hard it was for him to go to the Baron house."

"He went to the house?"

"Yes. I went with him."

Patrick didn't say anything. Clearly, he hadn't known about that.

"My brother isn't like anybody you've ever met or ever will meet, Miss Arley," he said after a moment. "He cares about people. And I don't mean just in principle. He's a doer—a fixer. He's been trying to fix me ever since he was a toddler. And I think he's trying to fix you, too. The one thing he can't fix is himself, and he needs to. He's got a lot of things he needs to get straight in his head, and neither one of us is helping."

"What do you want me to do, Patrick?"

"Leave him alone."

"No," she said, staring him down. "You have no right to ask me to do that."

"You do know he's going to be deployed. It's just a matter of time. He's got enough things worrying him, and he needs to be focused, not all torn up by some—" He stopped. "I hope you *don't* care about him. For your sake and his. What my brother needs, you can't give him, Arley."

"I don't believe I'm hurting him."

"If you're not, you will. This isn't about giving him what he wants. It's about giving him what he needs," he said, getting up from the swing.

"And you're the expert on what he needs, I guess."

"Yeah," he said. "I am."

"It must be nice to be so sure about things."

"I'm only sure about one thing."

"And what is that?"

"I don't want him to end up like me."

Arley thought he would go, but instead of leaving, he went inside. In a moment, she could hear him talking to Mrs. Bee. It occurred to her that he might have put himself into a twelve-step program since his recent episode, and he was taking care of one of the steps.

After a moment, he came out again. Arley looked at him as he passed, but neither of them bothered with goodbyes. She watched him leave and when she was about to go into the house, Scott's car pulled into the drive.

She walked out to greet her son, who bounded out of the backseat and gave her a big hug around the waist.

"I'm glad to see you, sweet boy," she said, returning the hug. "Did you have a good day at school?"

"Yeah, I'm going to like first grade better than kindergarten. You know that rock Will gave me? It's turquoise. Miss Bellingham told me. She said it was very creative to make up special names for my rocks, but I needed to learn the real names, too. She gave me a book—want to see?"

"We'll look at it tonight before you go to bed, okay?"

"Okay."

"Mrs. Bee's been baking," she said.

"Yay!" he said, dashing off to see what Mrs. Bee might have in her cookie jar.

Scott was smiling, possibly a genuine smile for a change.

"He's a great kid, isn't he?" he said, watching Scottie disappear into the house.

"Yes," Arley said.

"You get a lot of credit for that. You're looking…well," he added.

"Scott, what are you after?" she asked bluntly.

"Nothing. It was just an observation. I think you look nice, that's all."

She stared at him. In their entire marriage, she couldn't remember him ever spontaneously saying he liked the way she looked. She'd always had to drag compliments out of him and, quite frankly, she didn't know how to cope with two at one time—her mothering skills *and* her appearance.

"I repeat, what are you after?"

He laughed. "Nothing! I just think it's time we tried to get along—for Scottie's sake, you know?"

"I know," she said. "But I didn't think you did."

"I deserve that remark, I don't deny it. Maybe we can turn over a new leaf, though, for our son's sake. Don't you think?"

"Sure," she said warily.

He smiled again. "Got to go. I'll see you this weekend when I pick up Scottie."

She stood for a moment before she went back into the house, wondering what that was all about. The only thing that came to mind was something her father used to say—when somebody who doesn't like you starts being nice to you, look out.

But she didn't have time to worry about that now. She had to focus on her son, not on the distressing fact that Will was upset with her, or on what Patrick Baron had said, or on her nagging fear that she really might be bad for Will. She didn't want to hurt him. She wanted to be the best thing that ever happened to him. She went through the rest of the afternoon and evening hoping to hear from him, although she knew he was on duty. He'd managed a quick phone call before, and hope sprang eternal.

But her cell phone remained silent for the rest of the day and for the next two. On the third day she came home to find a load of lumber—pressure-treated logs—in the backyard.

"What are you building, Mrs. Bee?" she asked.

"Oh, it's not me. It's Patrick."

"Patrick Baron?"

"Yes. I've got a really big backyard and he's borrowing a little space."

Arley had her mouth pursed to ask for what, but Mrs. Bee handed her a piece of paper.

"Telephone call," she said.

Arley looked at it and frowned, wondering why the call came to Mrs. Bee and not to her cell. She didn't recognize the number. "The caller didn't leave a name?"

"No. She just asked for you. It's happened several times, so I thought I'd better check the caller ID—in case you might recognize the phone number."

A car horn blew in the driveway.

"Oh!" Mrs. Bee said. "There's Lula Mae. She's early. We're getting together with all the church ladies for award-winning movie night. Tonight it's *The Piano*."

"Mrs. Bee, you do know that movie is a little…"

"Oh, my, yes," Mrs. Bee said. "I know—but Lula Mae doesn't. Boy, is she going to be surprised."

"Mrs. Bee!" Arley chastised her. She was still chuckling to herself as she climbed the stairs.

"Look, Mom—chocolate chip," Scottie said of the cookie Mrs. Bee had given him. "Mrs. Bee is a good baker."

Clearly, she didn't have to hurry to get a meal cooked, so she set about straightening up the apartment and washing a load of laundry instead, keeping her cell phone close by, just in case.

It didn't ring until after she'd given Scottie a supper of macaroni and cheese and chicken strips, and after he'd had his bath. They were both lying on his bed looking through the rock hound handbook his teacher had given him when she heard her cell ring in the kitchen where she'd left it. It stopped ringing by the time she got to it.

She finished looking at the book with Scottie, then tucked him in for the night. Then she paced around the apartment.

Will was on duty tonight. And so was Kate.

She stood for a moment, thinking about who she could call. Mrs. Bee was out of the question. She and the church ladies were off watching *The Piano*. Gwen was also out of the question—she was always at a class of some kind or a meeting. And that left Grace.

She took a deep breath and dialed her number.

"Can you stay with Scottie for a little while?" she asked as soon as Grace answered. "I have something I need to do."

She expected Grace to say "Some*thing* or some*one?*" but she didn't. She didn't ask for details. She didn't say anything—at least, not to her. Arley thought she might have said something to someone there with her.

"Grace?" Arley said after a moment.

"Okay. I'll be there in a minute."

"Thanks," Arley said, marveling at how easy it had been and idly wondering if these newer aspects of two of her sisters' behavior indicated some kind of trend. She didn't quite know what to make of Gwen's new assertiveness or Grace's new acquiescence.

But she didn't have time to worry about the personality changes. She got dressed again instead. Not *too* dressed. She didn't want to provoke Grace into saying whatever she hadn't said earlier.

She opted for a face scrubbed clean of makeup, young matron shorts and a T-shirt right out of the clean clothes basket, sandals, and her hair in a ponytail. No designing woman here, she thought.

Grace arrived without delay, and she still seemed to have no sermons she wanted to deliver.

"I'm going to go to see Will for a minute," Arley said anyway, bracing herself to do battle. "I won't be gone long."

"Fine," Grace said.

*Fine?*

"Is Scottie asleep?"

"Yes. Grace?"

"What?"

"Thanks."

"I hope you're welcome."


"Are you still mad at my sister?"

"Ma'am?" Will said, startled by the personal nature of the question.

"I'm only asking because I see her getting off the elevator," Kate said.

Will looked down the corridor. Arley was making her way through the clutter of medical machinery lining the walls between the elevator and the nurses' station.

"Chow time," Kate said. "Well, go on. Take your break. She's not here to see me, regardless of what she might have said to the hundreds of people who have asked since she hit the checkpoint."

He put the chart he had in his hand back in the rack and went to meet Arley.

"Will," Arley began. "Can we talk a minute?"

"Let's go," he said. "I don't have much time."

"Where are we going?"

"To my place," he said, taking her by the arm and steering her in the direction she'd come.

"Your place is a barracks, Baron."

"Correct."

"I can go to the barracks?" she asked as he opened the stairwell door for her.

"If you sign in and leave before twenty-three hundred."

"Wow. Who knew?"

"You drive," he said. "Your vehicle's probably closer."

She kept looking at him as they walked toward the visitor parking lot.

"How much time have you got?" she asked as they got into her car.

"Thirty minutes, including travel time." He reached for her hand.

He told her which turns to make—using hand signals instead of verbal directions. She smiled at him at one point.

"Thank you. Very helpful," she assured him.

Unfortunately, Copus was manning the chest-high curved reception desk in the barracks lobby, and he did a monumental double take when Will and Arley walked in. He didn't clutch his chest and stagger backward with all the subtlety of a Redd Foxx, but he might as well have.

"Bring women here all the time, do you?" Arley said as they crossed the lobby.

"He'll be all right," Will assured her. "She needs to sign in," he said to Copus who for once in his life seemed to be at a loss for words. "Sometime this week, Copus?"

"Oh, yeah. Sign in. Right."

Copus got the book, giving Will a very significant and incredulous look in the process.

"Uh, Will?" he called as they were about to exit the lobby.

Will waved him off.

"Will!" he called again, and Will waved him off again. He could have executed a hopefully deterrent rude gesture behind his back, but Copus was notoriously unaffected by such things.

"So what do you think?" he asked Arley as they walked down the hallway, relieved that there was no beer bottle bowling in progress.

"It's not like I imagined. I thought it would be more..."

"More what?"

"More Gomer Pyle."

"That's the marines."

"Same difference."

"Don't ever let anybody in this place hear you say that," he said as he unlocked his door. He let her go in first, and she was waiting when he made sure the lock caught and turned around. She went immediately into his arms, catching him off balance so that they fell against the door.

His mouth found hers, and he kissed her hard. His hand slid up under her shirt to caress her breast and she made a soft sound, pressing her belly into his.

"We are—going—to talk, right?" she whispered between kisses.

"Right—" He lifted her off the floor and she locked her legs around him.

"I missed you…" she whispered.

"Whoa!" somebody said behind them. "My virgin eyes!"

Both of them froze. After a moment, Will carefully set Arley back on her feet.

"Sorry, man," the unexpected soldier said. "You must be my roommate. I…need to get out. Ma'am," he said to Arley as she stood back to let him open the door.

"I'm going now," he said. "But you should probably know I'm coming right back. With my mom. And my grandmother." He shrugged. "Sorry."

He left and closed the door firmly behind him. Will looked at Arley, and they both burst out laughing.

"Well," he said. "There is a good side to this."

"And what would that be?" Arley said, adjusting her shirt and smoothing the strands of hair that had come loose and fallen into her face.

"My reputation as a babe magnet just went up about two hundred percent."

She smiled and went into his arms again, kissing his cheek and then the corner of his mouth, and then his mouth. It took his breath away.

"I think we'd better go," she said.

"You want to see the rest of where I live?" he asked, for no other reason than that he wanted a memory of her being in it.

"Yes," she said.

He led her into his sleeping quarters. It was small, with dual-purpose pieces of furniture, including the bed.

"Nice," she said, walking over to look at the bulletin board. He had pictures of the Baron-Singer family on it. "Tell me who everyone is."

He told her, resting one hand on her shoulder. She briefly pressed her cheek against it and he was about a hair away from throwing her on the bed, mom and grandmother or no mom and grandmother.

"Have you got a view?" she asked, slipping from his grasp to look out the window.

"Just beautiful Fort Bragg," he said.

She turned to him again, going into his arms and resting her head on his shoulder. "You're not still mad at me, are you?"

"I wasn't mad at you. I was mad at Patrick. I was worried about *you*. It's one thing for my brother to cause the family all kinds of grief. You shouldn't have to deal with his crap."

She leaned back to look at him. "It's okay."

"Yeah?"

"Yeah."

He could hear the new roommate—or perhaps the old roommate he'd never met—returning. He could also hear women's voices as promised.

"Let's go make out in the car," Arley said and he grinned.

"Works for me."

"Baron, you still here?" the roommate called.

"Yeah," Will answered, letting Arley lead the way out.

"Ma'am," he said to the grandmother first as he had been taught to do, and then to the mother.

"Are you a relative?" the grandmother asked Arley with sharp-eyed interest when the introductions were over, making her grandson suddenly need to disguise a laugh as a cough.

"No, just a friend," Arley said. "We were just leaving—Will's got hospital duty."

"Nice to meet you," Will said to the women, following Arley's lead. "You'll have to sign out," he said to her as they hurried down the hallway. The clock was definitely ticking.

Copus was still behind the lobby desk, and he dutifully pushed the book in Arley's direction.

"I…tried…to…tell…you," he mouthed purposefully for Will's benefit as she signed.

Will looked at his watch. There was very little time left.

"Are you going to call me?" she asked as they walked to her car.

"Every chance I get," he answered.

"Will?"

He stopped walking because she did. "What?"

"I don't know where this is going—with you and me. But I know what I *don't* want. I…"

"What?" he said again.

"I like you. I like being with you—but I don't want this to turn into some kind of…serial…booty call— even if I did jump on you back there."

He looked at her for a moment, then drew a quiet breath. "Do you know I've told you more about my family than I've ever told anybody in my life? Does that sound like booty-call stuff to you?"

"No," she said, smiling slightly.

They stood looking at each other. A hot summer wind blew through the parking lot, and there was a faint rumble of thunder in the distance.

"Here," she said, scrambling in her purse. "Mrs. Bee gave it to me to take to work, but I never got a chance to eat it." She handed him a large cookie in plastic wrap. "Chocolate chip. It might be a little broken."

He smiled and took the cookie. "Thanks."

"You're welcome, Specialist Baron," she said, smiling and stepping close enough to lean against him.

He took that as an invitation and kissed her with much sincerity.

"Watch the PDAs, soldier," someone said sharply from a passing car.

"Sir, yes, sir!" Will said, without looking away from Arley Meehan's beautiful face.

## Chapter Ten

*Arley Meehan's beautiful face...*

"I brought breakfast," he said, holding up the paper bag full of sausage-and-egg biscuits so she could see it.

"Is that what they call it?" she said with just enough pointed mischief to rattle him.

"No. Yes," he said in spite of his determination to take a page from Copus's manual of seduction and stay smooth.

"It's very...early," she said, and she was working hard not to smile.

"That's when breakfast is—early."

"You just got off duty, I guess."

"I did. Yes."

"And you thought you'd drop by here on the off chance that I hadn't eaten."

"Correct."

"What's in the bag?"

"Sausage-and-egg biscuits."

"Ah. Maybe…you'd better come in then."

"Outstanding," he said, crossing the threshold. He held out the bag, but she didn't take it.

"Scottie's not here," she said, looking into his eyes.

"He isn't?"

"No. No school today, so Scott asked to pick him up early. He won't be back until Sunday evening."

When Will didn't say anything and didn't advance farther into the room, she took a step closer to him. "You must be very…tired."

"No," he said. "Not tired."

"You look tired to me," she said, coming closer still. "Actually, I don't think you can stand up much longer."

He grinned. "Now that you mention it."

She was close enough to nuzzle his cheek and she did. Her hair was damp, as if she'd just gotten out of the shower, and she smelled like…lemons and roses. "Drop the biscuits, soldier," she whispered.

He dropped the bag—and picked her up instead, staggering toward the bedroom with her, making her laugh when he didn't quite clear the doorframe.

"Sorry," he said, the laughter bubbling from his mouth into hers.

"No wonder…you come back…from field exercises so beat…up," she said between kisses.

"I want you to…know…this isn't a booty call," he said as they fell onto the bed.

"What is it, then?"

"This is me still missing you," he said suddenly serious.

"I've missed you, too."

He cupped her face with his hands and stared into her eyes. It was more than just "missing." He couldn't think about anything but her. She was the last thing on his mind when he went to sleep and the first thing when he woke—and he was afraid to say so.

"I'm glad you're here," she said.

"Are you?"

"Yes."

"Show me," he said.

She smiled slightly and began to kiss him, slowly and deliberately, as if they had all the time in the world.

"Show me," he said again, more urgently this time. He began to stroke her body with trembling hands. She didn't have anything on under the little dress she was wearing.

"Will…" she whispered.

"What?" he said between the kisses.

"Nothing…just…Will…"

And time ran out suddenly—to be replaced by sheer desperate need. He struggled to get out of his clothes. She helped until they were both naked, until they lay skin to skin, until there was no reality for him but her.

*So much better in a bed.*

It was a fleeting thought he couldn't hang on to. Like the leisurely concept of unlimited time, it, too, had been replaced and by another thought much more troubling.

*What if I love you?*

* * *

"Somebody waiting to see you," Trask said as Will crossed the barracks lobby, fully intending to sleep until he had to be back at the hospital. He was beyond tired and he'd never felt better in his life.

Trask nodded toward the conversation area in the far corner where Patrick sat sprawled on one of the easy chairs. With his usual nonchalance, he got to his feet and strolled over.

"Hey, bro. I need a favor."

"Yeah, and I'm just the person to ask for one of those—especially since we're on such good terms these days," Will said. "I don't have any money, Patrick."

"I don't want money. In fact, I want to pay you."

"For what?"

"I want you to do a ceremony. I want you to do the Blessing Way. For me."

Will stared at him. Of all the things his irrepressible brother might have said to him, this was completely unexpected.

"Are you drunk?"

"No. I'm…tired. I need help, bro. I want you to help me."

"Patrick, you know I don't do that anymore, and even if I did, you couldn't afford it. I get big bucks for that kind of thing."

"*Shich'i ahwii'na,*" Patrick said in Navajo—*It moves toward me,* the idiom for trouble, for a problem—or for Patrick himself, in Will's reality.

Will didn't say anything. Patrick had always been better at speaking Navajo, one of life's little jokes, because it suddenly occurred to him that maybe Patrick had never really wanted to live on the rez and had always wanted to be back here.

"*T'aa saho. Shik'ina'iilchiih*—" Patrick said, his execution of the language still perfect. *Alone...nightmares...*

"Patrick, I can't help you!"

"Yes, you can," he said in English. "I'm asking you, Will. I want the ceremony."

"And how am I supposed to do that? I'm not going to be anywhere near Window Rock for a long time."

"I'll take care of the details. I'll get the family to come here. I'll pay you your regular fee."

They looked at each other. In spite of Will's earlier thoughts, he could see that Patrick's coming to North Carolina had done nothing positive for him. If anything, he looked more the worse for wear than usual. A soldier who looked like he did at this moment would have been pulled from the line and set down hard.

"Are you going to make me beg you?"

"Patrick, I'm not doing it."

"Think about it. Will you at least do that?" Patrick said.

"There's no reason for me to think about it. I haven't done the Blessing Way in a long time. It's complicated. You have to get it exactly right. It's not something you can just pick up again at the drop of a hat."

"I know. That's why I asked Eddie Nez to come help you."

"Eddie Nez! Eddie Nez is a burned-out alcoholic. He doesn't have a brain cell left to remember who he is, much less the Blessing Way chant."

"And yet..." Patrick said with his usual maddening

insouciance. "He remembers, bro. He may not remember what day it is, but he's got that still stuck in his head. He taught you the ceremony and he'll come to make sure it's done right."

Will shook his head. Eddie Nez, who had once been Margaret Madman's boyfriend and who had let her hide the kidnapped child she didn't really want in his dilapidated trailer. It was his tenuous connection to Will's indifferent birth mother that had prompted Will to seek him out and negotiate payment for instruction in the Navajo healing ceremonies in the first place—another flagrant example of an ulterior motive, Will supposed, such as enlisting in the army in the mostly unacknowledged hope that he might find his real self in North Carolina.

But he hadn't seen Eddie Nez in years, and he didn't want to.

"And where is this supposed to happen, Patrick? You going to build a hogan in the courtyard out there?"

"No. Mrs. Bee's backyard, actually."

Somehow that didn't even surprise Will. If Mrs. Bee would help look for Patrick in a biker bar, she'd lend him a piece of her yard. The former schoolteacher in her couldn't resist having a cultural icon on the premises, if nothing else.

"You're going to build it all by yourself, I guess."

"If I have to."

"You are out of your mind."

"I know."

"You don't believe in this stuff, Patrick."

"No. But you do."

"Not anymore!"

"The Holy People come when you call them, Will. They come to you and Eddie Nez both. Everybody on the rez knows that."

Will didn't say anything. He looked down at the floor, and he realized suddenly that they had Trask's undivided attention and that Copus had joined him.

"We'll help you guys," Copus said as if he'd been waiting for the chance to put in his two cents. "Build whatever needs building. Right?" he said to Trask, who looked surprised.

But Will shook his head again and walked away, not realizing Copus had come with him until he was out the door.

"I think you ought to do it," Copus said trying to keep up. "Me and Trask both do."

"Thanks. I'll keep that in mind."

"No, I mean it—"

"Copus, you don't know anything about this, so butt out!"

"I know you got *something* going for you—how come everybody likes to jump when you jump, huh? Tell me that."

"I don't have a clue."

"It's because you got some kind of warrior thing going on. We can all feel it. When you jump, you do that chanting you think nobody notices and you move into some other place—into some kind of *zone,* man. You get the killer high and ain't nobody going to mess with you. Your brother's wanting you to do something like that for him, right?"

Will didn't answer him.

"He's looking pretty rough, William. You have noticed that? You know what I'm saying?"

"Yeah, I know what you're saying. What I don't know is why you care. I don't have time for this!"

"That's right, son. You don't have time. So you better not waste it."

Exactly, Will thought. What time he had belonged to Arley Meehan.

"Arley, somebody's wanting to see you out front."

"Okay," she said. She had heard the door alarm buzz—too early in the day for it to be Will dropping by for one of his brief hello-goodbye visits that she and the Head Start children had grown so fond of. Fond of the visit. Even more fond of the man.

In spite of her oldest sister and his half brother, Will was becoming an important part of her life. A welcome, if undefined, part. He often came to the apartment for usually wakeful lunches and suppers with her and Scottie, and sometimes she invited Mrs. Bee and Lula Mae and the rest of the church ladies. Arley really was good at making Tar Heel cuisine, and she loved showing off. She loved the attention Will paid to her son and the way he shared the Navajo fables about Coyote and the animals who managed to outsmart him. Sometimes he simply listened to Scottie's little-boy opinions and concerns, and not in the token, distracted way his father did. The three of them had gone on picnics and nature hunts in the park and in Mrs. Bee's backyard, and Arley couldn't help but see how relaxed Scottie was in Will's presence. Sometimes, Will seemed to recognize that Scottie was troubled about something even before she did.

She was relentlessly optimistic about the logistics of seeing him, in spite of the fact that he was constantly either working or training and that lately they'd only managed some brief conversations on the phone. She had told him the truth when she'd said she didn't want a purely sexual relationship—but she couldn't help wondering how strong her convictions would be if that were the only kind he was offering. At the moment, she was hoping that she and the specialist were going to have an entire uninterrupted night together, that somehow, some way, she was going to fall asleep and wake up in his arms.

She smiled to herself as she finished tying yet another untied shoe.

"There you go, Rickie. Thank you, Miss Arley!" she called after him as he dashed away, grinning to herself when he actually responded.

She went to the front of the building to see who had asked for her. A young woman who was dressed too businesslike to be one of the Head Start mothers stepped forward.

"Hi," the woman said cheerfully. "Arley Meehan, right? I've been looking for you everywhere."

"Well, here I am," Arley said. "Are you the one who's been calling Mrs. Bee?" It suddenly occurred to her to ask.

"Right. You've got one more crazy schedule. Here you go," she said, still smiling pleasantly and handing Arley some folded papers. "Have a nice day."

Arley looked down at them, then at the woman's retreating back. The door buzzed again as she walked outside.

Arley unfolded the papers, at first just skimming the words. But then she started over.

"Oh," she said out loud. "Oh, great!"

"Arley?" one of her coworkers said. "You okay?"

She shook her head no. She turned away so the children wouldn't see her face. Her hands were trembling because she suddenly understood Scott's compliments about how good she looked and what a good mother she was.

"What's wrong? Arley?"

Arley quickly folded the papers and stuffed them into her pocket. The war with the McGowans, the one Grace had been so concerned about, had begun and she couldn't make herself say it.

*He's trying to take my little boy.*

"I'm busy, Grace," Kate said. She moved the telephone receiver to her other hand. "Money for what? What! No, I don't have that kind of money. Well, when—no. Is Arley there with you?"

Will looked up at Arley's name, and, regardless of his dual-culture upbringing, he stood there flagrantly eavesdropping.

"Is something wrong with Arley?" he asked as soon as Kate hung up.

She glanced at him, and for a moment he thought she wasn't going to answer. "Yes. Her ex-husband had her served with a subpoena."

"What for?" Will said. "It's nothing bad, is it?"

"I don't know if it's bad or not. Scott McGowan always wants something—anything—besides what he's got. Grace says if it's about Scottie, they'd have to do a mediation first—they wouldn't be going straight to court. But I can't imagine what else it could be about." She gave a sharp sigh. "Here. Take care of this," she said, handing him a chart.

"Is Arley—?" he started to ask, but the look Kate gave him closed the door to further questions. He took the chart, and when he'd finished with the patient, Kate had left the unit for parts unknown. He didn't see her again until later, and he'd worked with her long enough to recognize that she still wasn't open to any questions. He tried to call Arley's cell phone the first chance he got, but she apparently had it turned off.

He tried again at the end of his shift, still without success. He decided to go to Mrs. Bee's in spite of the early hour. He found Mrs. Bee giving Scottie his breakfast in her big kitchen downstairs.

"Hey, Scottie," he said to the boy. "What are you eating?"

"Mickey Mouse pancake," he said around a mouthful.

"Good, huh?"

"Yeah! Really good!"

"Is Arley down here?" he asked Mrs. Bee quietly.

"No. She's still upstairs. Go on up."

"Thanks, Mrs. Bee," he said, turning to go. "See you later, Scottie."

"I'm glad you're here, Will," Mrs. Bee said, coming

to the kitchen doorway with him. She didn't say why and he didn't take the time to ask.

Arley's door was standing ajar. He rapped on it, then, after a moment, stepped inside. He could hear the shower running in the bathroom.

He could also hear some kind of noise down in the yard below and he walked to the closest window to look. Patrick, not known for being an early riser, was in the far corner near a stand of tall pines, picking through a pile of store-bought logs and two natural ones, one of which had a fork on the end. Apparently, Patrick was actually going to build a hogan. He had the skill to do it; it was his desire to do it that surprised Will. Patrick had finished his growing up on the rez, and he had been rowdy enough to have done more than his share of punitive community service. This wouldn't be his first Navajo building project, and drunk or sober or still half asleep, he was hard at work.

Arley was still in the bathroom, and Will went to the kitchen table and sat down. When she finally came out, she was fresh from her shower and dressed in shorts and a white T-shirt. He could smell the sweet clean scent of her soap.

She was startled to see him, but she smiled. Almost. He thought her eyes were red and swollen.

"The door was open," he said to make conversation. "The chair was empty."

She didn't say anything in response to his feeble wit, and he kept staring at her. She looked so vulnerable with her wet hair and bare feet. He had no doubt that she was worried and scared. Just like he was.

"I saw Scottie downstairs," he continued. "He was eating the ears off a Mickey Mouse pancake."

She smiled genuinely this time, but the smile quickly faded.

"Kate told me. About the subpoena—"

She didn't let him finish. She came immediately to him and sat down on his lap, her head resting on his shoulder. She gave a long wavering sigh as he put his arms around her.

"Grace tried to tell me he was up to something," he thought she said. "But I didn't think he'd—it can't be because of you and me." She gave another ragged sigh.

"Wait a minute," Will said, making her look at him. "Is that what Grace said? That I'm the reason Scott's doing this?"

"No," she said, but he didn't believe her. He already knew what Grace thought. She'd plainly told him the afternoon he'd fixed the dog pillow for Scottie.

But he asked the question anyway. "What did she say?"

"Nothing…"

"Arley, tell me what's going on. I mean it."

"I don't know what's going on. Not really. They tell you in the custody arbitration not to break the agreement. If you do, and the other parent can prove it…it could be bad. I haven't broken anything."

"So what's the complaint, then? The company you're keeping? Me, personally? My choice of careers? What?"

"Will, I don't know." She looked at him. "But I'm sure it's not *you*. I think anyone would do—anyone I was seeing. The specifics don't really matter. The

McGowans aren't very…particular when it comes to trying to arrange whatever it is they want."

"Yeah, I'm getting that. Well, that's that, then."

"What do you mean?"

"Arley, I can't be the reason you have to go through something like this. It's not fair to you or Scottie—I'm not even going to be here much longer. I can't cause you this kind of grief and then just leave you to deal with it—"

"I told you. *You* aren't the reason. Anyone would—"

"We both know better than that."

"Will…"

"I'm going," he said, lifting her off his lap so he could stand. "If I can help you with anything, let me know. Otherwise…" He didn't say otherwise what. He waited for a moment, then abruptly turned and headed out the door.

"Will!" Arley called after him.

"I can't, Arley!" he said.

"What, you're just going to dump me? Dump *us?*"

He didn't say anything to that, or to Mrs. Bee and Scottie on the way out. There was nothing to say—to anyone.

But when he reached the outside, he stopped for a moment on Mrs. Bee's porch. The sun was up. Kate had gotten home from the hospital. He could see her car on the other side of the hedge and smell the coffee her husband probably had waiting for her. He could hear the North Carolina version of birdsong and the buzz of insects, the little sounds, the *important* sounds of Mother Earth he'd been trying to teach Scottie to appreciate.

And Patrick was still dragging logs. A faint breeze

caused the wind chime hanging at the edge of Mrs. Bee's porch to tinkle softly, then it moved on and escalated until the pines swayed and gave a soft sigh.

Will walked in that direction. Patrick glanced up as he approached, but he didn't say anything. Neither of them did.

Will looked at the sky.

*Daltso hozhoni.*

All is beautiful.

Arley, how bad is it? he thought. Part of him wanted to believe that her fraternizing with somebody in the military—with *him*—couldn't possibly cause her any real trouble, that neither she nor Scottie were the worse for knowing him.

But another, more realistic part of him knew the truth. The McGowans owned the whole damned world, according to Copus, and that's all it ever took.

He bent down to take hold of the log Patrick was trying to move.

"Trouble—in—paradise?" Patrick asked as they struggled to stand it up on end so that it would slide into a deep hole he'd dug in the center of what would eventually be a hogan.

"None of your business."

"Right. Well, it's probably—for—the best. It's not exactly what—"

"Patrick, I'm telling you. You do *not* want to go there."

"Right," his brother said again, still grappling with the log—but clearly he had no intention of not saying what he wanted to say. "It's not like she could go live with you on the rez, bro. And I can't see you living here."

Will abruptly let go of the log and Patrick swore. "Why not?" Will asked, his tone of voice clearly a warning to be careful of the answer.

They stared at each other.

"Okay, bro," Patrick said finally. "It's...none of my business." He tried to pick up the log again, and, after a long moment, Will helped him.

"So are you going to do the ceremony for me or not?" Patrick asked when a second log rested in the Y fork of the one they had managed to get standing upright.

Will waited before he answered. All his training, from at least one of his worlds, suddenly came into play.

*What next?*

That was the question the army had taught him to ask himself in dire situations. What next?

He couldn't do anything for Arley. He couldn't do anything for himself. A blessing ceremony for his brother was all he could manage.

## Chapter Eleven

*He's not out there.*

Arley stood watching the activity in Mrs. Bee's yard—men building a more or less round structure near the pines. She had no idea what it was for, and the one person who would know she couldn't ask. There were at least three builders, not counting Scottie—who shouldn't be there, she suddenly realized. Scottie was supposed to be next door at Kate's watching the Saturday morning children's programming on her big television.

She hadn't seen Will since the morning he'd concluded that he was complicating her life and making her miserable. Both were true, but she had loved the kind of complications he brought, and she was miserable now because of his absence. She wasn't really surprised that he wasn't helping the others with the building project in the yard. She had stopped expecting to see him. She had tried for a time to be angry about his abrupt departure from her life, but she couldn't maintain it. At the moment, she was just…sad.

And hurt.

And worried.

She'd found herself a lawyer—the only one she could afford. The only problem was that the man looked ten years old. Even so, he'd assured her that Scott's attorney had gotten ahead of himself with the summons to go to court, that she and Scott could revisit the custody mediation without their respective lawyers first. He thought Scott and his prestigious law firm were just trying to scare her—which was definitely working.

She gave a quiet sigh and went downstairs to wrangle Scottie back where he was supposed to be. Halfway to the building site she realized that Cal was there working with the rest of the crew and that he had likely brought Scottie along with him.

"Hey, Cal," she said to her brother-in-law. "I thought I might need to get Scottie."

"No, he's fine," Cal said. "Muddy, but fine."

Arley thought she recognized one of the other men, a soldier she'd seen during her visit to Will's barracks. He was now wearing civilian clothes and wielding a shovel. He grinned suddenly, she supposed in honor of Will's new "babe magnet" reputation.

"Hi," she said to the soldier and to another man nearby.

"You can leave your boy if you want," the man said.

"He's a big help, actually. He likes mud better than we do. Don't worry. We'll watch out for him."

She glanced at her son, who was busily pouring water into dirt and getting wonderfully dirty in the process. She couldn't keep from smiling. "Are you sure?"

"Absolutely," the man said. "Besides making mud, that boy can name rocks like nobody's business—and we're only up to the brown ones—I'm Lucas Singer, by the way."

"Will's stepfather-uncle by marriage?" she said in surprise.

He smiled and extended his hand to her. "Among other things. Also Lillian Becenti's brother and…"

"The kick-butt lawyer," Arley said, and he laughed.

"I see Will's given you some of the family particulars."

"Some of them, yes," she said.

"So what do you think about all this?"

"This…?"

"About Will being a singer."

"A Singer?" Arley asked, still confused. He was a Baron. He didn't have his stepfather-uncle by marriage's name.

"The Blessing Way ceremony he's going to sing for Patrick."

"Oh, you mean being a *hataalii*."

"Yes," Lucas said. Clearly, it was his turn to be surprised. "Will's teaching you Navajo words?"

"Only that one. He's a…singer, then."

"That's one of the names for what he does. He's very good at it."

Arley nodded. That didn't surprise her in the least. "He said he'd stopped being one."

"Yes. He had—even before he went into the army. I think it's been a long journey for him to get back to it. I also think you might have helped him with that."

She looked at him. He had kind, observant eyes. "I didn't know he was going to do it."

She looked away for a moment. There was so much about Will she didn't know, so many things she hadn't had the time to find out. She realized that she had Lucas Singer's full attention, that he was studying her to determine what kind of person his stepson-nephew had gotten himself involved with.

"What was Will like—when he was a boy?" she asked suddenly, because it was important to know, somehow, and she might not get another chance to ask.

"Steadfast," Lucas said without hesitation. "Loyal to people who sometimes didn't deserve it."

Patrick came immediately to mind. Or perhaps he meant Will's birth mother. But then she thought that perhaps Lucas didn't mean Will's relatives at all. Perhaps he meant her. If he did, he was worrying for nothing. Will had removed himself from any and all temptation where she was concerned.

"You haven't talked to him lately," Lucas said. It wasn't quite a question.

"No."

"We haven't, either. The army is making sure he stays busy."

"Yes," Arley said. That reason was far better than the real one. She caught sight of another worker she'd missed seeing earlier—Patrick. She was still miffed at Patrick, and he with her, apparently.

"Will told you about me?" she asked Lucas.

"Yes," he said. "And Scottie."

She looked around at the sound of a car—Scott's. She couldn't keep from sighing. He wasn't supposed to be here today. He had his nerve; she'd give him that. Only Scott McGowan could have someone served with a subpoena, then drop by unannounced as if nothing had happened.

She didn't go all the way to the car to find out what he wanted. She took a few steps and then waited. After a moment, he got out and walked in her direction.

"We need to talk," he said.

"About what?" she said, choosing to be deliberately obtuse.

"About Scottie and my parental rights," he said. "You want to do it right here?"

"No, I don't. Not with Scottie six feet away," she said lowering her voice.

Only then did Scott seem to realize that their son was close by—and up to his elbows in mud.

"Is *that* a good idea?" he said, gesturing in Scottie's direction.

"I let him get dirty, Scott, so sue me."

"That's not as out of the question as you might think. This is no place for him—with these people."

"Who, Scott? His mother? And a…police officer?"

"Hello," Lucas said as if on cue.

"And a medic," the soldier in civilian clothes added helpfully in passing.

"I believe we've got it covered, Scott," Arley said.

"For how long?" he said. "You know how you are, Arley."

"I am a *good* mother!" Arley whispered vehemently.

"Been to any biker bars lately?" he asked mildly.

"What is *that* supposed to mean?"

"You know what it means. It says in the custody agreement that neither of us is supposed to be drinking while Scottie is in our care. *Care,* Arley. Not presence."

"*I* haven't broken the agreement!"

"Right. And G.I. Joe goes home to his little barracks bunk every night. You know you're just delaying the inevitable. There's no reason why we can't handle everything privately. You could be free to enjoy your budding…social life. You'll still see Scottie. A few minor adjustments and you could have alimony this time around—a significant amount. You wouldn't have to worry about money—"

"I'm not selling my little boy to the McGowans."

"You'd better think about it," Scott said. He looked at his son, who hadn't yet noticed his arrival.

"Hey, Scottie," he called. "What are you up to?"

"Clinking," Scottie called back without breaking the rhythm of his mud-stirring.

"Chinking," Patrick told him.

"Oh, yeah. *Chinking.*"

Scott clearly expected the conversation to continue, but Scottie was concentrating on filling a crack between the logs with his latest batch of mud.

"See you later, son," he finally called, and Scottie looked around briefly to smile.

"I'll see *you* in mediation," he said to her and walked away.

Arley had to fight hard to let the remark pass. Scott indicated his own degree of annoyance by displacing gravel the length of the driveway as he backed toward the street.

Thankfully, Scottie was oblivious to his father's exit and still happily making mud—something he'd likely never be able to do if he were under the McGowans' control.

She sighed again and turned her attention to Will's stepfather-uncle by marriage. It was too late to worry about what he might have overheard. "It was very nice meeting you, Mr. Singer," she said.

"My pleasure," Lucas said. His eyes met hers briefly, and she sensed that he wanted to say more, but he didn't, and neither did she. She had grown accustomed to long pauses in conversation from being with Will. Even so, this was probably her last opportunity to interrogate Lucas.

"I think you need to see Will do the Blessing Way ceremony," Lucas said when she was about to ask another question. "He was born to do it, whether he thinks so or not. It's a part of him maybe you need to know about. And I think it would mean a lot to him if you were there."

"I don't—"

Scottie gave a sudden squeal of delight behind her because Patrick was washing the mud off his hands and arms with the water hose. As soon as Scottie was passably clean, he raced past her and ran into the house.

"Potty break," Patrick said by way of explanation. "That pee-pee dance is a dead giveaway every time."

She smiled, then waited until Patrick was busy elsewhere. "Mr. Singer," she began.

"Call me Lucas," he said.

"Lucas." She took a small breath and made up her mind. "If you see Will, would you tell him...?"

They both looked around at the sound of voices coming from the street—raised and angry voices.

Arley immediately began walking in that direction, surprised that Scott's car was still partly in the driveway. He had gotten out—apparently to accost Will, who was also in the front yard but trying to walk away.

"You think I don't know what you're after!" Scott yelled.

"Give it up, Scott. I'm not going to fight with you," Will said, still walking.

Scott said something to him then that Arley couldn't hear. But she saw a familiar expression on Scott's face. She was worried now, and she intended to intervene before things got out of hand. But she didn't get the chance. Will stopped walking and whirled around.

"I want to marry her, you son of a bitch," he said, and Scott closed the gap between them, tackling Will in the front yard, both of them falling to the ground.

Arley meant to rush forward, but Lucas Singer caught her arm as both Patrick and the soldier who'd been shoveling dirt ran past.

"Scottie shouldn't see this," Lucas said, and she hesitated, knowing he was right. She stayed where she was, trying to watch the back door of Mrs. Bee's house for her son's return and the tangle of men on the front lawn.

Lucas Singer clearly had the experience it took to separate two men hell-bent on punching each other in the nose. The fracas was over as suddenly as it began— or it would have been if Scott hadn't said whatever he said at that moment. Will lunged at him, and Patrick and the soldier had to restrain him, then walk him bodily in the opposite direction, leaving Lucas to deal with Arley's ex-husband alone.

Arley stood there, not knowing who to yell at first. Did no one but Lucas Singer realize that Scottie was here, and that he did *not* need to see this?

In exasperation, she turned and abruptly went into the house to make sure Scottie didn't come bounding into the middle of it. She was halfway up the stairs when she realized the incredible words Will had spoken.

*I want to marry her...*

"You have *got* to work on 'smooth,' William. I'm mean to tell you, son—what the *hell* were you thinking?" Copus said, dragging Will into the patch of sunlight that was coming through Mrs. Bee's kitchen window so he could see the cut over Will's eye. "That was one more stupid, dumb-ass—"

"I know that, Copus. Just fix the damn cut."

"It's still bleeding a little, but I think we can butter-fly it—unless you want sutures."

Will gave him a look.

"Just checking," Copus said. "You do seem hell-bent on causing yourself all the agony you can these days— quit dancing around!"

Will tried to stand still. The initial adrenaline rush

was over, but he hadn't come down yet and his eye hurt. He needed to talk to Arley. He had to explain.

"I bet she didn't even know you wanted to marry her, did she?" Copus asked, completely undeterred by Will's combative mood.

Will didn't answer him.

"For somebody who plays it as close to the vest as you do, son, that was one hell of a big announcement, if you ask me."

"Nobody asked you!"

"Very true. Very true. You know, you kind of 'shock and awed' old Patrick and Lucas, too, while you were at it—not to mention your old buddy here. Hold still! See, I'm thinking we don't even know if her little boy saw you trying to punch out his old man. If he did, she might not want to talk to you—ever. Besides which, you're pretty scary-looking, Rocky—what with the eye and all. Damn, that was a stupid thing to do," Copus pointed out yet again.

"I didn't start it, and give me something else to worry about, why don't you!"

"I'm just telling you. All anybody saw was you and McGowan wailing on each other."

"Is my brother still here?" Will abruptly asked.

"Nope."

"Lucas?"

"Nope. You really know how to clear a backyard, I'll say that for you," Copus said, hunting for a butterfly adhesive in the first-aid kit from Will's truck.

*I want to marry her...*

Smooth, Will thought. He hadn't known he was

going to say it. All he knew—now—was that it was the truth and, for better or worse, it was out there. He gave a heavy sigh.

"You can say that again, son," Copus assured him.

Someone knocked at the door. Arley could hear muted shuffling in the hallway.

"Oh, great," she said under her breath. She didn't want to talk to her sisters. She wanted—needed—some time to think. But, clearly, she wasn't going to get it.

She took a deep breath, then flung open the door. "What!" she said to Gwen and Grace, who stood impatiently in the hallway.

"We hear you're engaged," Grace said pointedly. She had a red spiral notebook under her arm.

"Now, Grace, don't start," Gwen said, giving her a poke with her elbow. "Arley, you didn't tell us Will wanted to marry you," she said in a nicer version of the same remark.

"He doesn't," Arley said on impulse—in case they were fishing.

"That's not what he said," Grace informed her.

"How do you two know what he said?"

"Somebody named Copus told Kate—apparently he was an eyewitness—and she told us," Grace said. "Are you going to let us in or aren't you?"

"Oh, why not?" Arley said, throwing up her hands. "Where's Kate? Didn't she want to join the posse?"

"She had to work," Grace said. "Arley—"

"Does it matter to either one of you that I do not *need* this now?"

"We want to know what happened," Grace said. "For Scottie's sake, if nothing else."

"I think what you really want to know is how bad I messed things up."

"All right. Did you make things worse or not?"

Arley closed her eyes for a moment and waited before she said anything.

"Look. Scott and Will got into a fight. Will said what he said in the heat of the moment. You know as much about this as I do."

"You haven't talked to him?"

"No. I haven't talked to him."

"Where's Scottie?" Grace asked next.

"He's gone with Cal to get ice cream at McDonald's."

"Good. Let's get started."

"Get started with what?"

"Trying to figure out what Scott is going to do to you."

"Mrs. Bee will be here in a minute," Gwen said helpfully.

"Mrs. Bee?"

"We're going to sit down and try to put together what Scott thinks he knows," Grace said as if to someone who was two years old. "He must think he knows *something.* If you've got some idea of what's caused all this court idiocy, you'll be prepared. See?"

As much as Arley wanted to be left alone, she did see, and Grace was clearly in her element. She led the way to the kitchen table and tore each of them a sheet of paper, pausing long enough to order Arley to find some pencils so they could describe whatever came to mind about Will Baron and Arley Meehan and their decidedly bumpy relationship.

Mrs. Bee joined them after a time, and they all sat at the kitchen table scribbling away.

"I wonder if there's a detective," Mrs. Bee said thoughtfully at one point. "The McGowans have the money for one, and Arley said Scott knows about the biker bar."

"Well, how in the world did he find out about that?" Grace demanded. She had been so busy giving orders that she'd apparently missed the earlier, biker bar part of the discussion.

"Exactly," Mrs. Bee said.

"There's been a white car around," Arley said.

"What white car?" Grace asked.

"I kept seeing one—at my old apartment and after I moved here."

"Has Will ever spent the night when Scottie was here?" Grace asked. "Tell the truth."

"He's never spent the night, period," Arley said evenly.

"But the two of you are…" Grace glanced at Mrs. Bee and apparently stopped short of being her usual specific self out of respect for her.

"He dumped me. We aren't anything," Arley said.

"Right—except for that wanting to marry you part. What are you leaving out?"

"Nothing. I wrote down the biker bar," Arley said.

"Oh, yes. The little venture that only *looks* like you dumped your kid somewhere and went barhopping."

"I didn't dump Scottie! He was with his father—"

"Can you prove it?"

"I went to a bar with all of you!" Arley said indignantly.

"Yes, and I *told* you we shouldn't go in there," Grace said.

"That's right, Grace!" Arley said. "You did! But I did it anyway. You told me not to get involved with Will, and I didn't listen to that, either! Why don't you just say it, Grace! The McGowans are going to get Scottie and it's all my fault!"

She abruptly got up from the table and walked to the window to stand looking out at nothing.

*Oh, Will.*

He had actually told Scott he wanted to marry her— in front of Lucas and Patrick *and* her—when there had never been any talk of love, much less marriage. Never. She hadn't dared to even think about the "L" word.

Except whenever she looked at him.

And whenever she found him looking at her.

But she'd never *said* it, and neither had he. The sheer impossibility of their having that kind of relationship had always been understood.

Anyway, she thought, how could he be in love with her? He'd dumped her, walked away when the damage was already done, when she needed him and when his staying couldn't make things any worse. And he hadn't come back. That was the painful part. He hadn't come back.

There was a certain irony in it all, she supposed. She and Will both had been so careful not to let whatever was between them escalate into something that had to be defined, something that could break both their hearts.

And maybe they were going to suffer anyway.

tion, Copus had finally managed to part Will from a significant chunk of his pay. The bottom line was that Will
couldn't stand it any longer and he had to see Arley.

Had to.

He didn't want to talk to her on the phone. He didn't
want any secondhand reports. He wanted to know for
sure that she was all right. He wanted to tell her he
hadn't meant to cause her even more trouble with her
ex-husband. What he couldn't tell her was that he had
meant what he said. He did want to marry her, and he
didn't care who knew it. He kept thinking about the old
man who had sold her the ears of corn the day they'd
gone to the Baron home place. The old man had married
the woman he loved before he went off to a war—but
had he really known it was the right thing for him to do?
Will had no idea. All he had was relentless misery.

He walked in Patrick's direction, intending to do what
he'd ostensibly come for—to inspect the nearly completed
hogan. It had seemed sensible to have a token reason for
being here, and at the moment, he was glad of it.

All in all, the structure was…impressive. Patrick
and, he supposed, Lucas, had done a good job. They had
used the revised, early-twentieth-century form—a
hexagon of logs with a dome of mud for a roof which
wouldn't last in the kind of rains common in this part
of the country. The door opening faced the east, and
Will could see bits of turquoise and white shell and
obsidian imbedded around the facing. It was large
enough for the Blessing Way ceremony, and already
Will was visualizing the sand painting he would carefully create inside. Patrick clearly wanted his ceremony

done right, but how he was managing the expense of the hogan construction and what would amount to a complete relocation of the Baron-Singer family for the event was something else again.

Patrick stopped working and drove the shovel into the ground. "The sand for the floor came from the river-bank up by where Ben and Eden live," he said as Will knelt down to touch it.

It was white and washed clean. He didn't say anything because he and his brother didn't have real conversations these days. He had gotten past his anger after Patrick's bender, but he wasn't going to discuss his bold announcement that he wanted to marry Arley Meehan. Patrick had already voiced his disapproval of their relationship, and it was better not to go looking for aggravation. Will had agreed to do the Blessing Way for him, and he had managed to find some semblance of harmony in order to prepare for it. He was putting that meager harmony at risk just by coming to the place where both Arley and Patrick might be.

"Did you hear what I said?"

"The sand for the floor came from the riverbank up by where Ben and Eden live," Will repeated. He liked Eden and Ben. Eden was the daughter Lucas hadn't known he had until she was grown, and Will had done his part to help bring her into the family. She and her tribal policeman husband lived in a beautiful and peaceful place, and Will had done his purification rituals on the riverbank there many times.

"I still need some jet for the doorframe," Patrick continued. "Eddie Nez is bringing it and the pollen and cornmeal and the stuff for the sand painting. Oh, and the yucca for the ritual cleansing."

"You actually think he's going to get here with all that," Will said, unable to disguise his misgivings.

"The family is bringing him. If he's alive and breathing on the day of departure, they'll get him here and whatever you need."

Will smiled suddenly. If the Baron-Singer family had taken on the logistics, then a successful outcome was pretty much a done deal. He was looking forward to seeing everyone. In a perfect world, this would have been a good time to introduce Arley to them. And he would have introduced her in a way that they all would have known he was serious about her, and he wouldn't have been shy about it. He had already told Sloan a little about her—before Arley's legal trouble with Scott—in spite of the fact that he had no misgivings about the ultimate outcome of their star-crossed relationship. He'd answered all Sloan's invested female parent questions, knowing she'd pass the information on to Meggie and the rest of the family, and he hadn't minded. He had needed to tell them about what was happening to him.

But the world wasn't perfect. He'd learned that before he was Scottie's age, and he was still learning it. As much as he might want to, he wouldn't be taking Arley Meehan home to Arizona, wouldn't be showing her the places where he'd grown to manhood the way he'd shown her around a barracks room. It was clear to him now that he should never have mentioned her to anyone.

"You think the army is going to stay out of the way long enough for you to do this?" Patrick asked.

"So I hear," Will said, finally looking at him. He didn't say that the clock was ticking and that the rumors of imminent departure were rampant. "Most of my squad's coming."

"Why?"

"They want to."

"Your other family, I guess," Patrick said.

"Something like that. Some of them have kids, and they want them to see the ceremony."

"What about her?" Patrick said, jerking his head toward Mrs. Bee's upstairs apartment. "Is she coming?"

"I don't know."

"Is that why you're here? To hand-deliver her invitation?"

"No," Will said—because it wasn't. "I came to see the hogan."

He could feel Patrick looking at him.

"Sure you did," he said after a moment. "Lillian's coming to the ceremony, by the way. Maybe she can help. With Arley's court business."

Will didn't say anything. Lillian was the Navajo version of Arley's sister Grace. He couldn't see her helping in this situation, in spite of the law degree.

"It's not your fault Arley's ex-husband is trying to take her to court," Patrick said after a moment.

"It feels like my fault."

"It's *not* your fault," Patrick said again, reaching for the shovel handle. "You're taking this way too personal."

Will looked at him. "Has Lucas talked to you?"

"About what?"

"You know what!"

"You mean about telling Arley's ex and half the neighborhood you want to marry her? Yeah. He talked to me."

"What did he say?"

"He doesn't think you ought to."

"It's none of his business."

"Right. Let's tell him that so he can run along back to Window Rock and just forget all about it. And maybe you can forget what kind of family you're in while you're at it. Or have you already done that?"

No, Will thought. He hadn't forgotten. There was no such thing as an unaddressed problem among the Baron-Singers—even in Patrick's case, even when they weren't sure where he was. The whole family got involved anyway—and sometimes the tribe, too.

"Look, Will, this is your big bro talking. I know it bothers you—because of all the crap you had to go through with Margaret Madman. But this thing with Scottie and Arley is nothing like what happened with you and Margaret. Anybody can see Arley loves her kid. And Margaret…" Patrick didn't finish the thought. He didn't have to.

"It is the same from a kid's point of view. I lost a mother in a custody battle—whether she really wanted me or not. I know what that feels like. I know what it will feel like to Scottie if he can't live with Arley all the time. It leaves a big hole, Patrick, and you don't get over it."

"I'd hate for Sloan to ever hear you say that."

"Sloan understands that part of it. It's not…logical. It's…it is what it is." He gave a heavy sigh. "I'm a little worried about the noise," he said to change the subject. "The ceremony isn't exactly going to be quiet."

"Little Mrs. Bee has taken care of that. She and Scottie already went around to everybody in the neighborhood and told them what was going on. Then she invited them all to come. The *other* Meehan sisters are coming—Kate and Gwen. Even Grace."

"Grace who?" Will said because that surprised him, and they both laughed.

Patrick began shoveling sand again, and a car pulled into the driveway. Will looked around. It wasn't "Thelma and Louise" bringing Mrs. Bee and Arley back from wherever they'd gone. It was Scott McGowan in a very expensive...something.

"Damn," Will said under his breath.

"You're not going to go all ballistic again, are you?" Patrick asked.

"I didn't go ballistic the last time," Will said.

"Right. I was probably thrown off by all the blood."

"It was *my* blood, not his."

"Oh, yeah. I forgot. Didn't the army teach you anything?"

"Yeah. Don't go mixing it up with civilians," Will said.

"Well, so much for that."

Scott parked near Arley's car and got out, not seeing Will and Patrick until he had almost reached the back porch steps.

He was surprised to find them there, but he recovered quickly. He didn't say anything. He went up and rang the doorbell several times, ignoring them both.

After a moment, he came back down the steps and walked in their direction.

"Where's Arley?" he asked without prelude.

"I don't know," Will said.

"Now why don't I believe you?" Scott said, and Patrick stopped shoveling.

"Look, man," Patrick said, leaning on his shovel. "I wouldn't have a problem lying to you, but if my brother says he doesn't know, then he doesn't."

"Your brother?" Scott said with a laugh.

"You heard me," Patrick said, letting the shovel fall on the ground.

"Patrick," Will said, stepping between them as if Patrick had been the Baron hothead who ended up wrestling the man to the ground in a front yard brawl.

"You just tell her I'm looking for her," Scott said, glancing at the hogan. "Nice hut," he added and walked away.

"What do you think he's really up to?" Will said.

"Hard telling—but if I was Mrs. Bee, I wouldn't want him to know what day my pension check arrived."

"Scottie's not up here, is he?"

"No, Grace," Arley said with exaggerated patience. "He's downstairs with Mrs. Bee. She's baking for the church supper. He's going to look like he does after he's been in the mud pit—only with flour."

"I'm just asking, Arley. You've got a lot on your mind. I thought you might need a little help keeping up with the…details."

"Scottie isn't a detail I'd forget, Grace."

They looked at each other.

"I'm sorry," Grace said after a moment. "I know that. I didn't mean to suggest that you would. What's wrong?"

Arley sighed. And didn't answer the second of what would likely be a long series of questions. She was so *tired* of questions, especially her own.

"Arley?" Grace said, coming closer. Her voice was different suddenly. She sounded the way she had when Arley had been six and too afraid to tell anyone why she hid in the school bathroom during recess and wouldn't go on the playground. Grace had wanted the exact details then, too—so she could pound the reason for it into the ground. Kate had been the motherly one; Gwen, the most fun. But Grace had been the enforcer, the bodyguard.

"I saw Will," Arley said abruptly because she was reasonably sure Grace had no plans to pound him.

"What did he say?"

"I didn't talk to him. I just saw him. Out at the hogan. Working."

"Oh. Well."

"It was kind of…" Arley shrugged.

"Kind of what?" Grace asked when she didn't continue.

"Romeo and Juliet. Me up here, him down there. Looking at each other."

"Your families aren't feuding," Grace said, dismissing the whimsical notion entirely.

"If he'd meant what he said about wanting to marry me and we were going to do something about it, they probably would be. *My* family would be, and you know it. I keep—" Arley abruptly stopped because her voice broke.

"What?"

"I keep thinking if he'd just come tell me he didn't mean it. *Say* it—then we could both move on."

"He meant it," Grace said quietly.

Arley looked at her in surprise. "You think so?"

"Yes."

"Is that why you're being so nice to me. Because you think he means it and it's never going to work out?"

"Yes," Grace said again, reaching out to rest her hand on Arley's shoulder. "You could go talk to him, you know."

Arley gave a quiet sigh. "No, I can't." She looked at her sister. She wasn't a little girl anymore. She wasn't worried about the playground now. "I want him to mean it, Grace."

## Chapter Thirteen

Arley could hear the ritual chanting and the beat of a single drum, but she stayed where she was—alone in her apartment in the dark, watching from the window. She didn't see Will, but she knew he had to be there. This was going to be the all-night main event, the spiritual finale that was supposed to straighten Patrick out once and for all. Except that she didn't think Patrick wanted to be straightened out. She thought what Patrick really wanted was for Will not to go off to a war believing he hadn't done enough to fix his wayward brother.

And maybe Patrick was right. Maybe Will wanted to fix her, too. But what Patrick didn't understand was that "fixing" could be a two-way street. She had been

good for Will. She knew she had, and knowing that
made staying away from him now so much harder.

She walked to the window again. She could see
groups of people gathered in the yard, cooking foods
on charcoal grills and in what had started out as a hole
in the ground. Cars and trucks continued to arrive. She
could hear them cruising for a place to park somewhere
on the street. She hoped no one got too creative about
where they put their vehicles so that the ceremony could
be completed without police involvement.

She paced the apartment, straightening things that
didn't need to be straightened. Then she showered,
nibbled on cold leftover pizza, turned on the television
in time to see a woman in a pink ball gown and pigtails
sing opera to a man in a gray tuxedo. She turned the
television off, and suddenly there was nothing to keep
her from walking again to the window that looked out
over the backyard. This time, even in the waning light,
she immediately saw Will. He was standing in the
middle of a group of children, all of whom seemed delighted to have his attention. At one point, he looked up
at the window where she stood, and he kept looking.

*Romeo and Juliet.*

She abruptly stepped away and pulled down the
shade.

"You're the one who left," she said out loud. "You
can't just *look* at me and think I'm going to…"

But, unfortunately for her, he could. Her resolve
lasted only a few minutes more before she began
hunting for her shoes. When she found them, she
walked firmly to the door and opened it. There was no

reason why she shouldn't go see the ceremony if she wanted to. Her entire immediate family was somewhere in the yard below, and how much *more* heartache could her being there cause?

But when she reached the back porch, she hesitated. The night was hot and humid, and she brushed her fingers across her forehead as if it would help dispel the heat. She had never been the "when in doubt, don't" kind of person. She was the kind who looked after she leaped, after she damned the torpedoes, after she crashed and burned. She took a deep breath and began walking purposefully toward the hogan. There were two lines of people leading into it, one apparently for the men and the other for the women. She walked more quickly now, speaking to the people she knew along the way. There was good representation from the neighborhood, and Mrs. Bee's church ladies were very much in evidence. It suddenly occurred to Arley how much this seemed like Kate's wedding reception, only it was out of doors with a different kind of music. But it was still a collective goodwill event, a group of people coming together to share in someone else's life.

The lines began to advance slowly forward. Arley looked around for her sisters. She could see Grace and Kate ahead of her, but not Gwen, and she saw Scottie walking into the hogan with Cal and Lucas Singer. She got into the women's line. No one was talking.

The inside of the hogan was dimly lit, and it took a moment for her eyes to adjust. Eventually, she could see a large sand painting on the ground in the middle of the hogan. There was just enough room around the perimeter for the people to encircle the painting without marring it. A frail-looking man waited in what Arley assumed was a place of authority. There were bowls nearby and some carved and painted sticks and feathers.

And Will stood next to him, wearing a dark blue shirt, with a red bandanna tied around his forehead. The old man wore turquoise rings and heavy turquoise-and-silver cuff bracelets on each wrist, but Will's only jewelry was the strand of turquoise nuggets around his neck. She kept looking at him. He seemed so solemn—until he spotted her and, incredibly, he winked. She faltered in the line, surprised by the audacity of the gesture. He was behaving as if things were all right between them, as if she actually understood his glaring absence. The wink was pure Southern rascal, she suddenly realized. Something Patrick had probably taught him.

Will turned his attention to the old man beside him.

"See the sand painting?" a woman next to her whispered. "Will and Eddie Nez did that—Eddie's the one who taught Will the ceremony—after Will got him arrested for bootlegging, that is."

"He what?" Arley said, looking at her.

The woman smiled. "You'll have to get Will to tell you about that," she whispered. "The sand painting has to be done exactly right or the Holy People are offended and don't come. The symbol in the middle—with the face—that's Sun Father. Those triangles on each side of the painting are the four sacred mountains, and those are the Holy People," she said.

"Where?" Arley asked, only half listening, because Will had her attention.

"I can't point to show you—it's impolite," the woman said. "See? One is standing on each of the sides of the center square."

Arley nodded. Will seemed so intent, respectful and purposeful now. She had no doubt that he knew exactly what he was doing, and, she thought, neither did anyone else who was there, even the Holy People.

She looked around at the faces of the others, at her sisters, Kate and Grace—she finally spotted wide-eyed Gwen. Will's military friends were here, and, Arley supposed, most, if not all, of his Window Rock family. But she thought Will was no longer aware of any of them, including her.

Patrick was coming in. He was shirtless, wearing cutoff jeans and carrying a pouch. She made a small sound when he stepped boldly onto the sand painting and sat down in the middle of it, his legs outstretched, his hands resting on his knees. No one else seemed alarmed, but it was incredible to her that, after all the effort it must have taken to create the intricate design, it was acceptable for him to sit on it.

The ceremony grew more intense. Will was speaking to…

She didn't know. To her and the rest of the observers? To Patrick? To the Holy People?

She kept watching the two brothers. Something was happening; she could feel it even without really understanding. What she sensed, was Patrick willingly surrendering to his brother's ability to accomplish this—whatever *this* might be. Patrick seemed to be letting go and trusting that Will would catch him.

Will's chanting continued, and Arley began to lose all sense of time. She continued to watch him, to memorize him. She intended to keep this version of Will Baron in her mind and heart forever. She wanted him in her life, but the biggest obstacle to that—after the army and the McGowans and his culture and hers—was Will himself. There was no room for her and Scottie. None.

*Oh, Will!*

She needed to get out. She abruptly stepped closer to the hogan wall and began to backtrack until she reached the entryway. She walked blindly across the yard, and she would have kept going, gotten into her car and left if she could have, but Grace's car was in the way. She took a deep breath and climbed the porch steps instead, finally sitting down on the swing in the shadows.

The ceremony continued. The moon rose in the sky. She could no longer discern Will's voice. She was so tired suddenly—of the confusion, of the longing that threatened to overwhelm her. But she made no attempt to go upstairs to the apartment. The summer night was all around her, full of nocturnal sounds—tree frogs and cicadas and crickets. She nudged the swing slowly back and forth and she waited for...

For what? For her heart to break? For a chance to make a fool of herself? There was nothing she could say to Will. Nothing she could do.

She could see someone coming from the hogan—Grace carrying Scottie over her shoulder. After a moment, Arley stood and waited for them. Then she took her sleeping son from her sister and went into the house.

Will released the remnants of the sand painting and all the evil it contained into an early-morning breeze just as the predawn stillness gave way to the rising sun. He was exhausted. His eyes and throat burned from overuse.

"How do you feel?" he asked Patrick.

"Like I've been pulled through a keyhole backwards."

"Good."

"Is it?" Patrick asked. His voice sounded strained, as if he had been the one chanting for hours.

"Yes," Will assured him. He looked around Mrs. Bee's yard. Everything was more or less back to normal. Except for the hogan, little evidence remained that anything had happened here. The grass was a bit trampled, but that was all. Will let his gaze wander to the dark upstairs windows in Mrs. Bee's house.

"I don't think I would," Patrick said.

"Patrick, don't start."

Eddie Nez stood a few feet away, waiting, and Will walked over to stand next to him so that they could offer the final prayers and greet the new day. Patrick had been right about Eddie. Whatever else might have disappeared from his brain, the Blessing Way had not.

"I have something to tell," Eddie said in Navajo when they had finished. "About her."

Will glanced at him, careful to keep his demeanor respectful. "Who?"

"I cannot say her name."

Will frowned, aware of what Eddie's aversion to saying someone's name out loud could mean. But he didn't ask any more questions. Eddie had announced his intention. The burden was on Will to wait with patience and politeness until Eddie carried it out.

"You don't remember when she was beautiful," Eddie said after a long time. "You never saw her when her heart was good…before the alcohol took it all away."

Will glanced at him again. He could feel Patrick somewhere close behind him. They were doing this in tandem, he suddenly realized, this telling. He opened his mouth to ask something, then didn't. He had come very close to saying his mother's name out loud, and thereby summoning her ghost, her *chindi*, to come do evil to the living humans it had left behind. He was certain now where this was leading, but the question wouldn't go away.

"Is she dead?"

Eddie didn't say anything. His silence was enough.

"How did she die?"

"No one can say. Children playing at the chapter house found her by the side of the road. They think she fell down in the dark and hit her head."

"She was there a long time? Before anyone found her?"

"No," Eddie said, but Will didn't quite trust that answer.

"She was drunk," Will said. It wasn't a question, but he was still hopeful. He didn't want to think of her like that, drunk and dying on the side of the road.

Once again, Eddie didn't answer him.

"You were the best part of her," he said instead and Will gave a short laugh.

"She said that," Eddie said.

"Yeah, when?" Will said in English.

"When she knew I was coming here to help you do the Blessing Way for Patrick. She…"

"She what?"

"I think she knew what was coming. She told people she wanted her burial to be done the old way—in the red rocks. The people at the chapter house, they did that for her."

Will didn't say anything. He looked up at Arley's window.

"You were her son but she couldn't see you, Will Baron," Eddie Nez said. "No matter what you said. No matter what you did. She had no room for you, and she couldn't see you. But at the end, she did. It's better than never seeing you at all."

Will nodded, still looking at Arley's window. After a moment, Patrick clasped his shoulder.

"You okay?"

"Yeah. I'd…pretty much given up on her turning into June Cleaver."

"Not you, bro. You never give up on people. I'm proof enough of that."

Patrick didn't wait for him to respond. He and Eddie Nez walked away. But Will should have realized that he wouldn't be allowed to deal with this on his own terms.

Back at the barracks he slept a few hours, then reported for duty when he was supposed to. He volunteered to work longer than he was required because he needed to stay busy. He didn't want to think, and he most certainly didn't want to dream.

"Somebody's looking for you," one of the patients advised him when he had all but run out of excuses for hanging around the ward.

For one brief moment he thought, *Arley.*

But that hope died immediately when he saw Patrick walking toward him—steadily enough and obviously not drunk. But if he had brought some kind of problem, Will was too tired to deal with it.

"Come on, bro," Patrick said.

"Patrick, I don't—"

"Look, I know you're done here—in more ways than one. Let's go. I mean it."

"I don't want to go anywhere."

"It's not what you want, it's what you *need,* bro. I'll drive. Your truck," he added.

For whatever reason, suddenly *not* going back to the barracks and having to dodge a roommate didn't seem all that bad.

"Where are we going?" Will asked as they rode down Bragg Boulevard.

"Nowhere. That's the beauty of it."

But they did have a destination, one with a dirt parking lot and neon beer signs in the window. Will sat staring at the less-than-respectable-looking facade through the windshield.

"Well, that didn't take long," Will said finally. "The ceremony's worn off already."

"This isn't for me. It's for you. You need to let yourself go, bro. Have a few beers. Feel sorry for yourself. I'm here to watch your back."

Will started to say he was fine, that he didn't need

to feel sorry for himself, but Patrick had hit on the truth and Will was too exhausted to argue.

"What the hell," Will said as he opened the truck door.

"Now you're talking."

Will was met with a loud cheer when he opened the entrance door.

"William! You made it!" an obviously merry Copus yelled across the din. "Innkeeper! Bring my friend, William, and his brother here, your very, very… coldest…frostiest…cheapest brew!"

"Yeah, yeah," the man behind the bar said.

"Damn, Copus, how long have you been here?" Will asked him with an amusement that was tinged with concern.

"Not long enough," Copus advised him around a belch.

"Copus has got woman trouble," somebody said.

"I don't believe it," somebody else said in mock surprise.

"Yeah, dude. You should have seen the shortie he was with the other night."

"Was she good-looking?"

"Good-looking! Let's just say beauty is in the eye of the beer-holder."

Everyone at the table roared with laughter, and Copus chose not to be offended. "You better be catching up, William, that's all I got to say. Sit down! You've had your head up your ass long enough. The music is loud and the beer is cold—what more can a man want?"

*Nothing. Not a damn thing.*

Somebody grabbed two chairs from the nearest table.

Somebody else put a beer in Will's hand. And a third somebody began the obligatory "war" stories, which was constantly interrupted by corrections and put-downs from the circle of listeners at the crowded table. It had been a long time since Will had participated in one of these raucous, military versions of group therapy. The last one had concluded in a tattoo parlor on the Boulevard.

*Yes,* Will thought, *this is just what I needed.* And he was just fine with the good old country boy, sing-along music on the juke box, until somebody sent the mood in a different direction.

It was Van Morrison.

Van wanted to be *her* man, *her* lover. He wanted to be everything she wanted.

The name slammed into Will's brain, the longing, the need.

*Arley!*

## Chapter Fourteen

Arley stood in Mrs. Bee's laundry room, waiting for the spin cycle to start because the old washing machine couldn't be trusted not to walk itself out into the hallway. She looked around at a small sound, realizing that someone had come in the back door. She heard rustling, then footsteps, and then nothing. But whoever it was hadn't left, she was certain of that. She listened for a moment longer, then looked into the hallway, expecting anyone from a lurking private detective hired by the McGowans to try to catch her at something to an early-morning contingent of the church ladies.

But Will stood there in the wide hallway. He was wearing his uniform—BDUs. It occurred to her that a few months ago, she wouldn't have had any idea what this particular military ensemble was called. She couldn't tell if he was glad to see her or not. She kept waiting for him to say something, but he didn't. He looked…terrible, as bad as he had after the training exercises only without the cuts and bruises. He glanced away for a moment, his attention apparently taken by Mrs. Bee's kitchen doorway and the downstairs hall.

What's wrong, she almost asked, because she was certain that something was. Instead, she asked, "When was the last time you slept?"

Apparently the question was too difficult for him to answer.

"Are you drunk?" she said, because that was the only alternative she could think of that might account for the way he looked.

"Not so much," he said. "Now."

"You and Patrick go clubbing?" she asked. It seemed logical that Patrick would be in this somewhere.

Will frowned. Again he didn't answer her question. "Did you know that every morning we human beings get the chance to start over—to fix the things we screwed up the day before?" he asked instead.

"No."

"That's why we're supposed to greet the rising sun— because of what the Holy People said to First Man and First Woman. We greet the sun and we start over. It's a way for us to live with all the mistakes we were going to make in the Glittering World."

"The glittering world?"

"This," he said, gesturing to everything around him.

"I see," she said, but she didn't, not really, any more

than she understood why he'd stayed away. But, in spite of it, she was so glad he was here now.

He looked at her then. "I'm sorry," he said. "I'm not making much sense."

She had no argument for that. Mrs. Bee's washing machine kicked into its noisy and wobbling spin cycle in the laundry room behind her, and she turned her attention to that, opening the lid to make it stop. She stood there, staring down at the off-balanced wad of wet clothes in the still-spinning tub, the task of untangling them suddenly too complicated to attempt because Will had come to stand close behind her.

"I'd do anything for you," he said. "Whatever you needed. I don't want to hurt you. Or Scottie. Staying away seems like the best thing to do. Leave and stay gone."

She turned to look at him. "So what are you doing now? Coming or going?"

"I don't want you to think I was just using you—"

"What do *you* need, Will?" she interrupted. "Tell me that."

"You. I need you," he said without hesitation. "But it's—I can't—"

She reached out to press her fingertips against his lips. He needed her. That was enough. She didn't want to hear the caveats. She just wanted to keep him here, as long as she could have him.

"Did you have a good time?" she asked. "Doing whatever you've been doing?"

"No," he said. He reached out and put his hands on her shoulders and the sudden anguish she saw on his face made her lean into him and put her arms around him. She rested her head against his chest, feeling the starched roughness of his uniform against her cheek. Her eyes closed when he rested one hand on the back of her neck.

"I think you're here because you love me," she said. "That's what *I* think."

His arms slid around her, and he held her tightly. She could feel the pent-up tension in his body. He gave a ragged sigh against her neck, and she turned her head so that she could kiss his cheek. Once. Then again. She could feel him trying not to give in to whatever emotion she was eliciting.

Love?

She didn't know. She'd speculated that he loved her. He hadn't denied it.

She kissed his mouth, and he returned it. His kiss was soft and so sad—for a brief moment—and then the emotion—his emotion—swept over them both. He crushed her to him, his mouth hard and hungry. His hands slid under her T-shirt and she pressed her body into his.

"Will…"

But he suddenly gripped her arms and stepped away from her. "I can't do this," he said.

"Will, wait!" she called as he reeled into the hallway. He didn't stop.

She caught up with him, maneuvered ahead of him so she could get between him and the screen door. "What's wrong? Tell me."

She was in his way. He couldn't get past without touching her, and they both knew that wasn't a good idea. She reached out to him anyway, then let her hand fall.

"She…died," he said, his matter-of-fact tone belying what Arley could see in his eyes. "She *died*. Alone. Some kids found her on the side of the road. She was probably drunk. Nobody should die like that."

She didn't ask who he meant. There was only one person, she thought, who could cause him this kind of sorrow, the kind only someone caught in another person's hopelessness—or selfishness—could feel.

"She was the reason I wanted to become a *hataalii*. I wanted to show her I wasn't ashamed of the only thing she ever gave me—being half Navajo."

She waited for him to go on. "I'm so sorry," she said when he didn't.

"It was…I had a good childhood. Sloan and Lucas saw to that. And Meggie and Patrick. The whole family did. And the tribe. I shouldn't feel like this." He closed his eyes and shook his head.

She could see his despair, his regret at not having done something to prevent what happened—a ceremony, or one last effort to talk to the woman who had given him up so easily, one last attempt to persuade her to get the help she needed.

"Will…"

"I have to go."

This time she didn't try to stop him, but she wanted to wrap her arms around him and hold on to him as tightly as she could so he couldn't leave. But she didn't. She watched him walk away, and she stood at the screen door for a long time, listening to the tinkling of the wind chimes in the morning breeze.

\* \* \*

Will returned to the campground in the tall pines where the family had set up foldout tents and camper trucks for the duration of Patrick's ceremony. The scent of pine, dry summer dust and coffee hung heavy in the air when Will got out of his truck, but he barely noticed. His mind wasn't here, and neither was his heart.

"Back already?" someone said when he walked up.

He smiled at the mild joke because he hadn't talked to any of them since he'd done the Blessing Way. He was surprised—for a brief moment—that no one had left for home yet. Then he remembered the kind of relatives he had, and he was suddenly surrounded by his family, both real and extended, people who were proud that he was serving his country, who admired his ability as a Navajo singer, and who knew that he had been told about Margaret Madman. They thought his heart was heavy, and so it was, but not just for the woman who had given him life and nothing more. It was heavy because he couldn't find *his* way. He knew it would be a long time before they were all together again—if ever—and he still had to force himself to be there. He suffered their love and concern as best he could. He roughhoused with the children, accepted the food Sloan and his sister Meggie forced on him, and tactfully evaded answering the questions Lucas asked him.

He was there in body, but his mind and spirit were with the woman he'd just left. He had walked away—when he needed her more than he'd ever needed another human being in his entire life. The whole time he'd been trying to tell her about his good childhood, he'd been thinking how much he wanted to take her to Arizona to see all the places he called home.

*I do love you, Arley.*

And it was killing him.

*It's better this way.*

He would be leaving soon, and he might not come back. He had nothing to offer anyone, least of all her.

Nothing.

He suddenly looked up because Patrick had arrived.

Brother Patrick. Will's own personal exercise in futility. The other half of the Lost Brothers Baron.

Patrick would go back to wherever he'd come from, back to whatever place he arbitrarily decided to call home. All the family would go home, as well, and the one person he would miss beyond all reason would still be here.

"Hello," someone said at his elbow. Lillian. His irrepressible stepaunt by marriage.

"You okay?" she asked, reminding him of other times she'd asked him that. He couldn't match Patrick when it came to youthful indiscretions, but he'd had his share. And this was the woman who had come to his rescue.

"Yeah," he said. It sounded convincing—or would have to anyone but a kick-butt lawyer.

"You don't look okay."

He managed a small smile. "Actually, I've been up all night. Again."

She didn't say anything, but she was going to, and he had no way of heading her off.

"Are you serious about this woman?" she asked bluntly.

"Who wants to know?" he countered.

"Who wants to know?" she said pointedly. "Very cute, warrior-nephew. I can see you've been hanging out with Patrick too much." But she let it go. "I'll see *you* later."

She walked off, apparently to confer with Lucas about something.

Will stood for a moment, then sighed because Patrick was coming in his direction and Will had no hope of escape.

"You're okay with it, then?" Patrick asked, looking at him closely.

"Okay with what?"

Patrick puffed out his cheeks and blew.

"Okay with what?" Will asked again.

Patrick seemed to be considering his options, and Will could tell the very moment he decided to hell with it.

"The court thing."

"Who's going to court?"

"You are, bro."

"Me!"

"Peacemaker court. The family wants it. They're worried about you—"

"I am *not* going to peacemaker court," Will said, realizing suddenly why everybody from Window Rock was still here. He was also struck by the fact that he'd had this same conversation before with Patrick, only he'd never been on the receiving end before.

"I would if I were you," Patrick said. "Believe me, it's a whole lot easier to just get it over with."

Until now, the less-than-repentant Patrick had been the reason the Baron-Singers needed the Navajo version of family counseling, and Patrick had hardly been a willing participant. Will had been to several of these sessions and each of them had had the same goal—reforming Patrick. "Peeling the onion" is what the process was called, because of the tears that were almost always the result.

"I don't need to go to peacemaker court!" Will said.

"This time it isn't about what you need," Patrick retorted. "It's what *they* need, so you and the army had best get your scheduling ducks in a row. One way or another, you're going to have to go because Arley's the reason for it—"

"Are you kidding me?"

"Do I look like I'm kidding? Believe me. *Nobody* is kidding. What did you expect? You're the one who made the big announcement about wanting to marry her."

"This is *my* business."

Patrick didn't say anything. He only stared at him, and Will swore.

"Who's the tribal representative?" It suddenly occurred to him to ask.

"Lillian," Patrick said, and Will couldn't help but laugh at the absurdity of Lillian Singer-Becenti taking on the roll of "peacemaker."

"She thought you'd be more comfortable if she presided."

"I'm not going," Will said.

"Yeah, I think you are, bro. They're holding it in Mrs. Bee's dining room."

## Chapter Fifteen

Kate was waiting on the top step of Mrs. Bee's stairs when Arley got home from work.

"What's the matter?"

"I need to talk to you," Kate said as Arley juggled groceries and unlocked her apartment door. "Where's Scottie?"

"Where he's supposed to be. With Scott. Unfortunately."

"You know, it's good the way you do that."

"What?"

"You say 'unfortunately' to me, but you'd never say anything like that to Scottie."

"No, I wouldn't. He loves his father," Arley said, wondering what this visit was really about.

"Here," Kate said, handing her something that looked like a small wadded-up piece of newspaper.

"What is it?" Arley asked.

"It's from Will. He said to give it to you and tell you to be strong."

"Is he all right?"

"When it comes to paratroopers, that's something just about impossible to find out."

"Is he all right?" Arley asked again.

"I…guess he is. The army is working his butt off—part of the master plan for keeping the troops from obsessing about imminent deployment."

"I thought—"

"What?" Kate asked.

"I thought he'd…call or something."

"This is the 'or something,'" Kate said, still holding out the small wad of newspaper.

Arley took it and turned it over so she could remove the paper. It was a piece of turquoise that had been shaped into the form of a bear.

"It's a fetish. You're supposed to carry it with you when you go into battle," Kate said. "He says the Navajo may have stolen the idea from the Zuni—he's not sure."

Arley stared at it. "He's the one going into battle," she said, but she clutched the fetish tightly in her hand.

"There are battles and there are battles," Kate said obscurely.

Yes, Arley thought. The mediation was next week and the clock was ticking. She looked around because she could hear voices downstairs—not the church ladies, she decided, since some of the voices were male. "I wonder what that is?"

"That would be the other kind of battle," Kate said. "The one Will's concerned about. He's going to be here in a—"

"Here? Will's going to be here?" Arley interrupted.

Kate ignored the inquiry. "—but he doesn't have much time. He was afraid he wouldn't be able to explain it all to you."

"All what?"

"His family is taking him to court—a peacemaker court. It's a Navajo thing. They have concerns—"

"What kind of concerns?" Arley asked, and Kate gave her a pointed look.

"Me?"

"Apparently."

"I don't understand."

"Well, nobody is happy about the possibility of you and Will getting married."

"Is that so," Arley said, immediately insulted.

"You know it is."

"I suppose nobody has noticed we aren't even seeing each other?"

"No, we only noticed the part where he told your ex-husband he wanted to marry you. His family has this peacemaker ritual to voice concerns about family matters—to get everything out in the open."

"You mean, *now?*"

"Roger that," Kate said.

"Wait a minute. Will's family is having some kind of meeting downstairs?"

"Yes."

"About me?"

"Among other things," Kate said vaguely.

"And this is just fine with Will?"

"I don't think he had much to say about it."

"Why are they doing it here?"

"My guess is it's the one way to get him to partici-
pate," Kate said.

"Well, *great*," Arley said, heading back for the door.

"Where are you going?"

"To court," Arley said.

"You can't go," Kate assured her.

"Well, I'm not going to stay up here and wait for my
ears to catch on fire." She threw open the door. Gwen
and Grace were standing in the hall. "Excuse me," she
said, pushing past.

"Where are you going? Where is she going?" Arley
heard Grace ask. But she didn't hear the answer. She
heard three sets of footsteps clunking down the stairs
behind her.

"We can't go, can we?" Gwen asked.

"No, we can't," Grace assured her.

Arley thought she heard Will's voice and she
abruptly stopped, causing confusion in the ranks behind
her. Of course she couldn't just barge into whatever
this was. She didn't want to embarrass Will—or her
sisters, either, for that matter. She gave a sharp sigh and
sat down on the stairs. All three of her sisters sat down,
as well—where they could hear everything said in the
dining room. Unfortunately, they could also be seen by
anyone who happened to come near the doorway.

"Well, this is certainly subtle," Grace said.

"It's better than pushing our way in," Kate said.

"Shhhh!" Arley said. "I can't hear!"

She couldn't see, either. She had no idea how many people were in Mrs. Bee's dining room. All she knew was that Will was one of them.

Someone was calling the meeting to order—a woman.

"There will be no raised voices," she was saying "None. Patrick, since you're not the focus of this session, I'm assuming we can keep the swearing to a minimal."

"I don't know, Lillian," Patrick said. "Will knows the same swearwords I do. And probably some I don't."

There was a pause. A long one. Arley imagined the look Patrick must be getting from the kick-butt lawyer.

The woman said something Arley couldn't hear. Then she began speaking—in what Arley assumed was Navajo—and a few moments later, switched to English again—for a prayer.

"Will," the woman said. "Meggie couldn't be here. She had to get back to Window Rock. She wrote down some things for you to read. But we're here, and I want to thank you on behalf of the family for the respect you've shown us by coming—"

Arley couldn't hear Will's response because the front doorbell buzzed. The sisters all looked expectantly at Arley, but she wasn't about to walk past the dining room to answer the door, for all her former bravado. Fortunately, Mrs. Bee came bustling out of her kitchen into the hallway. The unanticipated sight of all four

Meehan sisters perched on her staircase gave her pause, but she didn't say anything. She continued to the front door. Grace leaned out to see.

"The mailman," she said.

But Arley wasn't interested. She was trying to catch more of the conversation in the dining room.

Mrs. Bee came back down the hallway with a folded letter in her hand.

"Arley, this is for you," she whispered from the foot of the stairs. "Mr. Perkins found it in the bushes just now. He said he delivered it weeks ago."

Arley came down the stairs to get it. The letter had been everything but spindled and stapled. She turned the envelope over. *Custody/Visitation Mediation* was still clearly visible in the return address.

She tore the envelope open and began to read.

"Oh, no," she said after a few lines.

"What is it?" Grace whispered.

"Oh, no!"

"What?" at least two sisters said in unison.

Arley looked at them. "They changed the time for the mediation. I missed it!"

"Arley, how could you possibly miss it?" Grace cried.

"Oh, for heaven's sake, Grace," Kate said. "You just saw how."

"What are you going to do?" Gwen asked.

Arley stood there, staring at the letter, registering only that the custody mediation appointment had been last Friday. The name of the mediator finally came into focus—and this was something that had to be addressed right now.

"I'm going to see if I can talk to somebody," she said. She looked at her sisters who were rising to their feet. "No. I want you all to stay here. If you get the chance, I want you to put in a good word for me. If this peacemaker meeting is about me, I ought to have a chance to get in my two cents. I want you to say I'm a good person— because I am. I want you to tell Will's family that I love him—no matter what they think, no matter what *anybody* thinks. I want you to do that for me."

All three of her sisters stared at her; for once, even Grace was silent.

"I mean it," Arley said. "If Will's family cares about my part in this, I want one of you to say all that for me. Or all of you—so it will sound like the truth. Because it *is* the truth. Please."

"Okay," Gwen said after a moment. She gave Grace and Kate a hard look.

"Okay," the three women said more or less in unison.

"Okay," Arley repeated. "I'll be back when you see me."

She looked in the direction of the dining room before she rushed upstairs to get her purse and car keys. Her sisters were still sitting on the stairs when she came back down.

"Thank you," she whispered, patting each one on the head as she squeezed past and ran out the back door.

She knew where she needed to go, but finding a place to park was something else again. By the time she got to the office suite where the custody mediations were held, she had just missed catching the mediator before he began another session. There was nothing for her to do but wait.

She went back out into the hallway because there was no place to sit, and she ended up standing close to the wall, out of the path of the parade of people milling around or passing through. Some were chatting and laughing. Some swore. One wept openly. Some, like Arley, simply tried to endure.

She clutched the turquoise bear tightly in her hand, and she worked to drag her thoughts away from the Bee dining room peacemaker court. She kept thinking about Will. She hadn't seen him since the morning he'd told her about Margaret Madman's death. His family must have seen the way he looked then, too. If they had, it was no wonder they wanted to have a meeting.

She opened her purse and took out the battered letter, then put it back again. This was a waste of time.

Will could hear Mrs. Bee's grandfather clock ticking somewhere in the house, the only sound that penetrated the growing silence around the table. Silence was acceptable in the Navajo culture, but this particular lull had passed uncomfortable and was barreling toward excruciating.

Will glanced at his family members—Patrick, Lucas and Sloan, and Lillian who was serving a dual tribal leader/family role. The letter Meggie had written was still lying unread on the mahogany table in front of him.

Someone was coming down the hallway and he looked around to see Mrs. Bee carrying the pitcher of iced tea she'd promised. Arley's sisters followed in her wake, each woman bringing something—a tray of ice-filled glasses, a plate of cookies and a bowl of sliced lemons, and starched and ironed embroidered napkins.

"Thank you, Mrs. Bee," he said.

"You're welcome, Will. It's the way you like it," she added as she placed the pitcher at the head of the table by Lillian. She left the room immediately.

He tried not to smile as Arley's sisters placed the rest of the refreshment items next to the pitcher of tea—because he knew why Gwen had been assigned to carry the napkins instead of something breakable.

"Kate," he said when the sisters were about to leave. "Where's Arley?"

Gwen started to answer, but a sharp nudge from Grace shut her down.

"She's not here, Will," Kate answered. She didn't elaborate, and he didn't press her. If Arley had decided not to hang around while his family discussed her at length, he couldn't blame her.

Except that no one attending the peacemaking had discussed anything at all so far.

Kate and the rest of the sisters left, and Lillian began pouring glasses of iced tea. Will waited until everyone had their glass, until the cookie plate was passed around, until he had read Meggie's letter.

Sister. Little mother. Friend. Meggie.

*Do you remember when Patrick was in his Lynyrd Skynyrd phase and drove us crazy listening to the same album all the time?* she wrote. *Well, sometimes things that drive you crazy can come in handy. (I'm talking about a song here—not Patrick.)*

Will chuckled softly to himself.

*This song says everything Sloan and I both want to say to you, our darling Will.*

He kept reading. The rest of the letter was song lyrics. He recognized them immediately. They were from "Simple Man," a fervent hope that a young man would find love and live well, the Lynyrd Skynyrd version of walking in beauty.

He looked up from the letter and directly into Sloan's eyes. She didn't look away, and neither did he. Patrick was right. It was better to just get it over with. He took a deep breath before he spoke.

"I can't find my life," he said.

Kate and Gwen and Grace were sitting on the stairs where Arley had left them.

"Did you find out anything?" Kate asked. Her whispering indicated that the peacemaking must still be in progress.

"I found out I had to talk to my lawyer about rescheduling." She looked from sister to sister. "*Well?*" she asked. "Did you tell them what I said?"

"No," Kate said. "They're still—"

"I wanted to," Gwen said. "But—"

"We didn't know if you really meant it or not," Grace interrupted.

Arley let her purse drop with a heavy thud on the bottom step and walked in the direction of the dining room.

"Wait! Wait! Will's not there," Kate called after her just when Arley reached the doorway.

Arley stopped short, but it was too late to backtrack.

She stood in the doorway, looking at Will's family, at Lucas and Patrick, at the woman presiding at the head of the table—the one who had explained the sand painting to her the night of Patrick's ceremony—and finally at the attractive woman sitting next to Lucas, the woman who must be Sloan, the most beloved of Will's four mothers.

No one said anything.

"Will had to go," Patrick said after a moment, and Arley nodded. She realized that her sisters had come to stand behind her and that they were in rescue mode, but Arley didn't leave. She waited for what she hoped was a polite interval before she made her statement, addressing them all.

"I love Will Baron," she said. "Now what are we going to do about it?"

## Chapter Sixteen

Arley stayed late after work, trying to finish a blur of paperwork for an upcoming audit and helping with the janitorial duties for the Head Start building because there was no one else to do it. It was nearly dark and raining by the time she finally got home. She ran from the car to the back porch without realizing someone was sitting in the swing.

Will.

She stopped short, startled. She didn't say anything. She stood looking at him, her heart pounding. It took everything she had not to fling herself at him, whether he was actually here to see her or not.

"Thank you for the bear," she said, because that was the first safe topic that came into her mind.

"You're welcome."

"I needed it—when I had to reschedule the custody mediation. They changed the appointment date and the letter got lost—well, it ended up in the bushes, so I didn't know the date had been changed and I missed it—and that didn't look good. But I think it's going to be all right. I've got enough witnesses—Mrs. Bee and the mailman. They know I didn't just blow it off—" She stopped because she was babbling. She waited for him to say something, anything.

"Your turn," she said when he didn't.

"I'm an idiot," he said.

"Oh. Well. Did you…come to that conclusion all by yourself or did you have help?"

"I had help."

"Anybody I know?"

"The list is pretty long."

"I'll bet," she said, and he smiled.

But the smile faded and he lapsed into silence again. There was just the sound of the rain and the tinkling of the wind chime.

"I'm going to go in for a minute and see Scottie. Don't leave, okay?"

"Okay," he said.

She ran into Mrs. Bee in the hallway.

"He fell asleep watching a Pokémon video. He's on my bed," she said.

"Thanks, Mrs. Bee," Arley said, giving the old lady a quick hug.

She took the shortcut through the kitchen to Mrs. Bee's bedroom at the front of the house, and she saw a

silver-framed photograph lying on the kitchen table—
a man in uniform, Mrs. Bee's first husband, Bud. Arley
had always loved hearing the story of Bud and Mrs.
Bee. Mrs. Bee had met him on a bus, a young paratrooper on the fast track to a world war. Mrs. Bee had
thrown caution *and* her family-approved fiancé to the
wind in order to marry Bud. A whirlwind courtship, a
wartime quickie South Carolina marriage, and then
nothing. Bud had gone off to war and hadn't come
home again. Mrs. Bee still held memorial dinners for
her lost soldier.

Arley tiptoed quietly into Mrs. Bee's bedroom,
thinking as she always did that it looked like something out of a 1940s movie—except for the television
and VCR. Scottie loved lying on the puffy satin com-
forter and throw pillows and watching a video when he
stayed with her—a very risky thing to let a little boy
who basked in mud and dirt do.

Arley stood by the bed for a moment, watching her
son sleep, then bent down and kissed him gently on the
cheek. Dot, his beloved dog pillow, lay close by, her
sutured chin very much in evidence. Arley gave a quiet
sigh and quietly left the room.

"Arley?" Mrs. Bee said as she came back through.
"Wait just a minute, will you? How are you, Arley?" Mrs.
Bee stood holding the silver-framed photograph, and the
question was so…kind and full of concern that Arley had
to wait a moment before she trusted herself to answer.

"I'm…I don't know how I am, Mrs. Bee."

"It's good you talked to Will's family."

"Is it?"

"Yes. They needed to see you, talk to you. Scottie likes Will, you know."

"Does he?"

"Oh, yes. He's already put Will on the list. He's very proud to have someone on it."

"What list?"

"The one at his school—of soldiers who are already or about to be deployed, for the children from the different classes to send letters and care packages. I understand a few sailors and marines have managed to get on it, as well," she said with a smile. "Scottie and I are kind of partial to the paratroopers, though."

Arley smiled in return. *So am I,* she thought. "I'll be back to get Scottie in a little while."

"Arley?" Mrs. Bee said when she turned to go. "You know you don't have a lot of time, don't you?"

"Yes," Arley said, realizing that Mrs. Bee wasn't referring to how long Scottie could nap on her bed. She touched the pocket in her skirt to be sure she had the turquoise bear before she stepped outside onto the porch. It was still raining. She half expected that Will wouldn't be there, but he was sitting on the swing where she'd left him. She didn't join him; after a moment, he got up and walked over to her. They stood watching the rain, not touching, listening to raindrops splatter on the trees near the porch.

"Female rain, isn't it?" she said.

"Yes."

"It's an interesting idea—"

He reached out and took her hand, his fingers warm and strong around hers.

"What are we going to do, Arley?"

She drew a quiet breath. "I asked your family that," she said, smiling slightly because of the incredulous look her remark caused. "What, you think the peace-maker court adjourned just because you left?"

"I…had hopes," he said. "What did they say?"

"They don't know. Nobody does. Not even us."

"I love you," he said quietly, and her heart leaped.

"I know you do—and so do they," she said. "And I love you. But we're not a good match, Will."

"No. We're not."

"Except for the love."

"Yeah, there's that," he said.

She looked at him. "I…"

"What?" he asked when she didn't go on. She reached into her pocket with her free hand and closed her fingers around the turquoise.

"I don't know anything about the army. I don't know anything about Arizona or the reservation or the Navajo. It's all a…big mystery to me—with you standing smack in the middle of it. The only thing I know is…" She stopped. "This is harder than I thought."

A car turned into the driveway, its headlights cutting a swath through the rainy darkness. But, whoever it was didn't stay. The car backed into the street again and drove away.

She waited a moment before she continued, before she lost her nerve. "All I know is I could put Scottie and everything I have—everything I am—everything I ever will be—my *heart*—into your hands right now—and not…be afraid—" She had to stop because she was going to cry. She took a deep breath and tried to stop her bottom lip from trembling, then bowed her head because she was losing the battle.

He pulled her into his arms and held her tightly. "I never know what you're going to say. Never—don't cry."

"I can't help it. We don't have a lot of time, do we?"

"Oh, about five days," he said, and she looked at him in alarm.

"Five *days?*"

"Four, maybe. I'll be penned up the last day or so."

"What if something happens?" she said. "What if I never see you again—"

"Don't," he said. "Don't."

"I *hate* this," she said, holding on to the front of his shirt. "I hate it."

"It would be a crazy thing to do," he said.

"What would?"

"Us getting married."

"I'm Arley the Handful. Believe me, no one would be surprised."

"Except you and me."

"Except you and me," she agreed.

"Arley?"

"What?"

"I think we could make it. I've seen marriages that aren't supposed to work, work anyway—Lucas and Sloan, and Meggie and Jack. They couldn't be any more mismatched, but they love each other and they respect each other. They're *kind* to each other, even when maybe they don't feel like it. I love you, Arley—more than I can ever tell you. I love who you are and the way you care about your sisters and Scottie—the joy you give other people without even trying."

"I'm afraid it's not just joy, Specialist," she said truthfully, but he wasn't deterred.

"I love that part, too," he said. "I've been looking for the place where I belong for a long time—only now I think it's not a place at all. It's a person. It's you. I don't have much to offer—it's not easy being a military wife. But I want us to get married. Now. Before I leave."

She leaned back to look at him. "Okay," she said easily. If he expected to have to talk her into it, he was going to be disappointed.

"It's going to take some doing," he said.

"Okay," she said again.

"No, I mean, *you'd* have to do it. Make all the arrangements. Everything. I think I could get to the courthouse for the license, but that's about it. It would still be up for grabs whether or not I'd be able to show up for the wedding before I'm deployed."

"Okay," she said yet again.

"And there's Scottie. I don't want to be the reason his life gets turned upside down. I won't be here to help if Scott keeps at you."

"I have some very formidable sisters," she said, making him smile. "And I think it'll be alright with Scottie. Mrs. Bee just told me he's got you on the list."

"I don't know what that means," he said, but another car turned into the driveway before she could explain. This time it stayed, and the driver blew the horn.

"That's Copus. I've got to go. I'll call you when I can," he said. "If I can. Are you sure you want to marry me?"

"I'm sure." She smiled suddenly. "Don't worry. I'm pretty good at on-the-job training."

He laughed and hugged her. Hard. She kissed him once and then again. They broke apart at the sound of running, splashing feet behind them.

"Let's go! Let's go!" the soldier yelled, and Will bounded down the steps.

She ran to the far edge of the porch, realizing that this would likely be a big part of any life they made together—watching him leave.

"So be it," she whispered.


"Will and I have to get married…" She was going to say "in four days," but all three sisters suddenly looked at her belly. "No! We don't *have* to get married—we have to get *married*—right now if we're going to do it before he's deployed. And you have to help me."

"Is that what you called us over here for? Well, you can count me—"

The sisters turned their collective attention to Grace.

"In!" Grace said defensively. "You can count me *in!* I know I had objections—I still do—and I personally think you're crazy—but since when did that ever stop you from doing whatever you want to do? Besides, that peacemaker court helped. A little bit, anyway, because apparently you understand your situation better than I thought you did. So I'm in."

"You mean it?"

"Yes, I mean it."

"Grace, thank you. I need you to figure out a way for us to get the marriage license. It'll have to be done on the run. Will's family is still here—they're doing some work at the Baron house while they're waiting for him to be deployed. Somebody may have to break the news to them if Will can't. And the wedding can't be anything fancy—I don't have time for fancy. It just has to be something Will can get to."

"We could do it at the hospital chapel," Kate said. "We've had some ceremonies there. I'll get the chapel reserved—and the chaplain, if you want it army. Of course, he'll try to talk you out of it first. The army doesn't want anybody rushing into marriage."

"I just want it legal," Arley said. "As for talking me out of it, the chaplain has missed his chance. The peacemaker court is over."

"I'll handle the food," Gwen said.

"Food?"

"You can't have a wedding without food and drink, Arley. Don't you worry. I've got it covered."

"Okay," Arley said doubtfully. "Okay," she said again, feeling better than she had since the marriage became an actual possibility—if there was such a thing—in spite of Gwen's threat to handle the refreshments. "I've got to go see Mrs. Bee—I'm going to invite her and the rest of the church ladies. All of them can play the piano, so they'll have the music covered—and if there isn't a piano, they can…hum 'The Wedding March.' I'll be right back."

She left her sisters in a huddle. She really did want to talk to Mrs. Bee. But she needed to talk to Scottie first. She found him rolling miniature vehicles around the potted plants near the screen door.

"Hey," she said. "I need to ask you something."

"Okay," Scottie said, still rolling cars. "What?" he added when she didn't say anything. She didn't know quite how to start, and she decided to just say it.

"Will and I want to get married, and I want to know what you think about that."

"Yes," he said.

"Yes, what?"

"I heard Aunt Kate say it to Mrs. Bee—Will wanted to marry you."

"So what do you think?"

"He'd be a husband, right? He wouldn't be my dad. That's what Jeffery said."

"Jeffery from school?" she asked, wondering how long Scottie had known about this.

"Yeah. His mom's got a husband and *he's* got a dad."

"Will would be my husband, yes," Arley said.

"Would he live with us?"

"When he's not doing army things."

"Cool."

"Cool?"

"Yeah. He'd be handy to have around. In case anybody needed su…"

"Sutures," Arley supplied.

"Yeah. Or I got scared or something. He likes me. And you," he added as an afterthought.

Arley smiled. "Who told you that?"

"He did."

"He did?"

"Yeah. I said I liked you the best of anybody in the universe, and he said, 'Me, too.' Mom, you're in the way of my yellow car."

"Oh, sorry. Well. I guess I'll just…run along."

"Okay. Can we have macaroni and cheese for supper?"

"Macaroni and cheese it is," she said. She walked away a few steps, then came back to kiss him on the top of his head. Several times.

"Yikes," he said with a giggle as he always did when she got carried away.

She laughed and went to find Mrs. Bee, who was delighted, and not surprised. When Arley went back upstairs, she found Kate coming out the door, Grace making a list and Gwen looking for a cookbook.

"Later," Kate said, giving her a quick hug in passing. "And good luck."

Arley had no doubt that she would need it. Will had been serious when he said she'd have to do everything. With Grace's help, Arley and Will managed a few minutes together to get a marriage license and a few minutes of some serious kissing on the sidewalk. Arley and Will both had to talk to the chaplain, as warned, in spite of the intensive counseling they'd both already been through with their families. If Will was having any second thoughts, Arley certainly couldn't tell.

On day four, at 1800 hours, Arley was all done up in the ivory-colored linen sheath dress Kate, Grace and Gwen had bought for her and waiting at the hospital chapel with Scottie, her sisters, Lucas and Sloan, Mrs. Bee, Lula Mae, and the church ladies. Arley didn't know where Patrick was, and she refused to worry about it. Will was the one she was worried about. There couldn't be a wedding without the groom, and she was so nervous she could barely breathe—so much so that Kate and Sloan both took turns reminding her.

"Take a deep breath!" Kate said for what must have been the tenth time.

"All right! He's late."

"Well, yes," Kate admitted.

"Why is he late?"

"I don't know. I'll…go see what I can find out."

She left the chapel as Patrick wandered in. He was actually dressed for the occasion, and Arley tried to take some reassurance from that.

"Where's the groom?" he asked mildly.

"You didn't expect to see this day happen, did you?" Arley asked instead of answering.

"Day ain't over yet, Miss Arley," he said, and she looked sharply away.

"No, wait, wait," he said, coming closer and putting his arm around her shoulders. "I'm sorry. I didn't mean that."

"He's late, Patrick," she said. "I don't know where he is."

"Well, he's not going to miss getting married, I can promise you that. *I* might blow off my own wedding, but he wouldn't."

"Don't be nice to me! I know how you feel about this. I'm nervous enough as it is—and quit laughing."

"I'm not laughing—well, yeah, I am. A little. It's never easy with you two, is it? Anyway, I want my brother to be happy, and I think you do, too. That's good enough for me. Okay?"

She remembered to breathe. "Okay."

"Here comes Kate," he said.

"Did you find him?" Arley said, hurrying to meet her. "Oh, don't tell me. He's changed his mind," she added because of the look on Kate's face.

"The good news is he's upstairs. The bad news is he's working and he can't leave."

"What do you mean he can't leave?"

"He can't leave—they're expecting a bunch of new patients to arrive—any minute. He's got to help get them all situated. Me, too, actually."

"Well, that's it, then. We can't take the wedding to him."

"Funny you should mention that," Kate said, nodding toward two soldiers, who were clearly patients, waiting just outside the chapel door. One was in a wheelchair with both legs extended. The other was attached to a bag of IV fluids on a pole that he was more or less using to hold himself up with.

"Ma'am," the standing soldier said to Arley. "If you'd come with us."

"Where are we going?" Arley asked.

"Elevators, ma'am. Everybody else move out," he announced. "Go to the stairwell. Proceed up the stairs to the next floor but do *not* exit the stairwell, clear?"

The guests looked at each other, then nodded.

"Outstanding. Sir, if you would accompany the bride, sir," he said to the chaplain. "I also need the best man and the chief relative who is giving away the bride."

"Over here."

Patrick and Scottie came to join Arley.

"Can't do this without us, can they?" Patrick said.

"Nope," Scottie answered.

They couldn't do it without the groom, either, Arley thought in dismay.

"Excellent," the soldier who was clearly in charge said. "We have a unified purpose and we *will* prevail, hooah?"

"Hooah," Scottie said, perfectly at home in this conversation.

Both soldiers looked down the hallway. And looked. Arley looked at Kate—who shrugged.

"I have to go," she whispered. "See you in a bit."

"Ma'am," both soldiers said as Kate squeezed past them and hurried away.

"What are we waiting for—?" Arley started to ask, but the most vocal soldier held up his hand to stop her, his attention still on something down the hall.

"There it is," the other one said.

"Roger that. Ma'am, let's move out."

Arley moved out, following Patrick and Scottie and the chaplain to the elevators. The rest of the wedding guests walked to the stairwell entrance where another soldier was posted.

"Are we going to get Will into trouble?" It suddenly occurred to Arley to ask.

"Not in the plan, ma'am," the walking soldier said, punching the elevator button.

"Damn," the medic closest to Will said when the elevator doors opened. "*Who* is *that?*"

"*His,* that's who," Copus advised him. "So watch it."

"Nice," the medic said with far too much enthusiasm.

"What did I just tell you!" Copus said. "Ignore him, William—but, *damn,* you are a lucky, *lucky* man."

Will nodded, and kept standing where he'd been told to stand—in front of a commandeered bed table that had been draped with a draw sheet decorated with white ribbons and a big potted peace plant—right next to the stairwell. He could hear people coming up the steps, and Copus opened the exit door with flair. He didn't let anyone come onto the floor, however, and he began taking great pains to position people where they could see.

Will smiled at Sloan who had, just a few hours ago, set him straight once again about his perceived obligations to her, to the family and to the tribe. "It's one thing to end up with a broken heart because you tried something risky and failed. It's something else again if your heart's broken because of regret. Lucas and I don't have any regrets, and I don't want you to have any, either. No matter what."

One of the nurses handed Arley a bouquet of pink carnations, tea roses and baby's breath—the nursing staff's contribution to the wedding ceremony.

"I'll be damned," the medic who had already admired Arley said. "You guys really *are* having a wedding."

Will didn't bother to answer. His attention was on the bride. She stood by the elevators until Copus gave her escorts the signal to let her advance.

Will couldn't stop looking at her. He had always thought she was beautiful and today she was…outstanding. She smiled, and he took a deep, grateful breath.

*Mine,* he thought.

Word of the Plan B wedding had spread up and down the hospital corridor. Patients were doing their best to get their wheelchairs and crutches into the doorways so they could see the bride making her way to the make-shift altar. For some of the patients, it was the first time they'd been out of bed today. Hopefully, nobody would pass out from the exertion.

At a signal from Copus, Arley's military escorts sent the chaplain and Patrick forward.

"Sir, can you get this done in six and a half minutes, tops?" Copus asked the chaplain when the man got to the end of the hall.

"I can, Specialist Copus," he said, belying his earlier determination to talk Will and Arley out of doing something in haste, dictated by a deployment.

"Then we are good to go, sir," Copus said, giving another hand signal.

A guitar player positioned in one of the doorways began to strum a soft tune, and Arley took Scottie by the hand and began to walk slowly toward where Will was standing and the chaplain waited with his open book.

"Arley, you stand here. Will, right here. Patrick, Scottie. Can everyone hear me?" the chaplain said to the people in the stairwell. A couple of the church ladies moved closer.

"Who gives this woman to be married?" he asked, bending down so Scottie would know that was his cue.

"Me!" he said, transferring his mother's hand to Will's.

"Thanks, buddy," Will whispered.

"You're welcome," Scottie answered.

"Come help me hold the ring," Patrick said, and the boy went to stand beside him, placing the wedding ring that had once belonged to Sloan's mother, the woman of the beautiful Christmas trees, carefully on his thumb.

Will looked into Arley's eyes. It was really going to happen.

"Hurry this along, sir!" he heard Copus say.

Yes. Hurry.

"Go to sleep."

"No," Arley said, lying beside Will, unwilling to take her eyes off him in spite of the soft darkness of the room, unwilling to waste even a moment of the time they had left. She'd sleep later—when she had to sleep alone.

"You sleep," she said. "I'll wake you in plenty of time."

But clearly he didn't want to sleep, either. He gathered her into his arms and buried his face in her neck. His hands moved over her body.

"I love you, Will," she whispered. "And stop worrying."

"I'm not worrying."

"You're worrying about what Scott's going to do—at the custody mediation."

He didn't say anything, and she reached up to rest her hand gently against his face. She didn't tell him about Grace's theory—that the "lost" custody mediation letter had been the reason Scott had accosted Will that day in Mrs. Bee's front yard. That he must have been trying to get rid of it, but Will had arrived and Scott hadn't known how much Will had seen, how much he realized. And Scott had resorted to his usual tactics when he was caught in the wrong. He went on the offensive.

"Lillian's offered to come and kick his butt legally if I need it," she said. "And if that doesn't work, Gwen's enrolled in a karate class."

"Poor Scott," he said, and she laughed softly.

His arms tightened around her.

"I want a baby, Will," she whispered.

Her cell phone abruptly rang, and he swore. They both knew that a phone call tonight—this morning—couldn't mean anything good, regardless of which one of them it was for.

Arley switched on the lamp and climbed over him to answer it. "For you," she said, handing him the phone, watching him make the instant switch from bridegroom to steely-eyed military man. The message from the NCO on the other end was apparently short and to the point.

"I have to go," he said, tossing the cell phone aside.

She moved to sit beside him. "I guess we're lucky to have this much of a honeymoon," she said, leaning her head briefly against his shoulder, hoping he couldn't hear the slight quiver in her voice.

"It's more like a miracle," he said. "Arley, I don't want you to come see me off—"

"I'm coming," she interrupted. "Scottie, too. Some of the wives are swinging by to pick us up so we don't get lost."

"It's not going to be much."

"I don't care. I'm going to stand at the fence with the rest of the families and watch you walk to…whatever."

"You do know we all look alike," he whispered, and she smiled—briefly.

"I have to be there, Will. I *have* to. I don't think I can stand it if I don't…" She stopped, determined not to cry. The seasoned military wives who had helped Gwen serve surprisingly good wedding cake and punch to an entire medical unit after the ceremony, had also briefed Arley on one of the most important aspects of wifely deployment behavior: don't bawl all over him.

So she wasn't going to. She hoped.

She lay back on the pillows, watching as he put on his warrior garb.

He smiled at her. "That's the way I want to remember you," he said. "Just like that."

"Okay," she said, smiling in return and trying to find her mischievous self somewhere in the misery that threatened to overwhelm her.

He sat down on the bed. "You've got the phone numbers."

"The entire population of Window Rock, I think," she said.

"Don't worry about what you hear on the news, okay? They'll tell you soon enough—if there's anything to tell." He looked at her. It took everything she had not to cry. "Okay?" he asked again.

"Okay," she said.

"Kiss me—hard," he said and she scrambled to him.

She kissed his mouth and his eyes, and he lifted her across his lap and lay her down so that he could kiss her belly.

"In case our baby's in there," he said.

She wrapped her arms around him and kissed him one more time, and then she let him go.

## Epilogue

*B*reathe...

She took a deep breath, and then another, hoping to make the light-headedness fade away. This time, she didn't have Scottie with her and she didn't have to stand behind a fence—homecomings were clearly a different animal, particularly this kind.

"Are you okay?" Patrick asked because she hadn't wanted to rest before she went to the hospital.

"Yes. I'm just...hot," she said in spite of the snow on the ground. Her cheeks felt flushed, but her hands were so cold. She kept looking around her. She had barely noticed the sights of Washington on the way in and now there was nothing to see. "Tell me again," she said as they walked toward the hospital entrance. She shifted her shoulder bag because it was so full of things people had given her to help her get through this. Scottie had contributed a stack of pictures he had drawn. Horses. Lots of horses because he knew Will used to ride them when he was on the reservation.

"His right leg is broken," Patrick said, his voice calm and matter-of-fact.

"From being shot?"

"Yes. He had surgery to fix that in Germany. He's got two more wounds, one in the other leg and in his left arm. Those are minor—their words."

"But he's all in one piece?"

"Yes."

"Why didn't he get out of the way, Patrick?" she asked, on the verge of crying again.

"You know why—because he's Will Baron. He wouldn't leave a wounded man, no matter what."

"How does he look?"

"Thin. Drugged-up. But he's still our Will—go that way," Patrick said.

"I'm…glad you're here," she said, and he nodded. She didn't ask him anything else. She just kept walking and trying to remember to breathe. She kept her eyes straight ahead, so as not to process where she was and why she was there.

"Wait here," Patrick said.

She waited while he went to a nurses' station and spoke to one of the nurses. The woman immediately came out from behind the desk and walked in Arley's direction.

"Let me go in first for a minute, Mrs. Baron," she said, smiling. "Then it's your turn."

Arley and Patrick waited in the hallway. The nurse didn't stay long.

"Okay," she said. "First bed on the left. He's a little out of it, so be prepared. And he's a hardhead—those guys from the 82nd take being the kids your mama wouldn't let you play with to heart, don't they? He's lucky to be home—but he doesn't know it yet."

*Be prepared,* Arley thought. How does that work?

"I'll be down there—in the waiting room. I'm going to call Window Rock," Patrick said, and she nodded.

She was finally going to see Will, and she didn't hesitate. She knew what to expect—or she thought she did.

She saw him immediately. His eyes were closed. His right leg was in a complicated-looking metal splint. His left leg and arm were heavily bandaged. He had tubes in his right arm.

*Minor.*

She walked to the bedside and reached out to put her hand in his. His fingers felt warm and dry—and oblivious.

"Will?" she said softly, because there were other beds around him, all of them full.

"Will?" she said again, squeezing his hand.

He opened his eyes. "Hey…" he said. He smiled, but he had to work at it. The smile faded and he frowned. "Get Nelly," he said.

"Nelly?"

"The nurse…get her…"

"Okay," Arley said with some alarm. She backed away and hurried into the corridor. She saw the nurse standing in the doorway of another room.

"He wants you to come," Arley said.

The nurse walked back with her, moving ahead at one point to enter the room first.

"What's up, Specialist?" she asked briskly.

"Help me," he said.

"I need more to go on than that, Will."

He motioned for her to come closer and said something to her Arley couldn't hear.

"Roger that," she said.

She immediately began to raise the head of his bed. "Get over here, Mrs. Baron. The specialist has plans for you."

Arley stepped close to the side of the bed, realizing after a moment what he intended. She dodged the IV tubing so he could put his almost free arm around her. He raised up as much as he could and held on to her tightly. Then he kissed her, the pain it caused him apparent. He let go and fell back on the pillow, then looked at Nelly and pointed downward. She lowered the bed until he said stop. With Nelly's help, he raised up again and embraced Arley. This time, he placed a kiss on her ever-growing belly and the baby girl who still had two months to go. Arley wrapped her arms around Will for a moment before he lay back against the pillows.

"Now," he said. "*Now* I'm home."

*  *  *  *  *

The Man Who Had Everything, *the next new
novel from beloved Special Edition author
Christine Rimmer will be published
next month, July 2008.*

*As one of our special centenary editions*
The Man Who Had Everything *will have
some extra features from the author and
a bonus free story!*

*Here's a special sneak preview…*

# The Man Who Had Everything
## *by*
## *Christine Rimmer*

Stephanie entered the barn, the bright sun outside lighting her gold hair from behind, creating a halo around her suddenly shadowed face. Grant, his senses spinning, somehow managed to get his boots under him and rise from the bale.

She came right for them. "Hey, you two. Mom said I'd find you out here." She reached him, slid her warm, callused hand into his and flashed him a smile. "C'mon. Got some things I want to show you."

Prickles of awareness seemed to shoot up his arm from the hand she was clutching. Her scent taunted him: shampoo, sunshine and sweetness. It took a serious effort of will not to yank her close and slam his mouth down on hers—with Rufus sitting right there, fingering that cigarette he hadn't quite gotten around to lighting yet.

*This is bad. This is...not like me,* Grant reminded himself.

And it wasn't. Not like him in the least.

Yeah. All right. He knew that in town, folks considered him something of a ladies' man.

And he did like a pretty woman. What man didn't? But he never obsessed over any of them, never got tongue-tied as a green kid in their presence.

Not until today, anyway.

Stephanie. Of all the women in the world...

By some minor miracle, he found his voice. "Show me what?"

"You'll see." She beamed up at him, those shining eyes green as a matched pair of four-leaf clovers. "Come on." She tugged on his hand.

He let her pull him along, vaguely aware of a chuckle from Rufus behind them and the hissing snap as the cowboy struck a match.

Inside, she led him to the office, which was off the entry hall, not far from the front door. She tugged him over to the desk and pushed him down into the worn leather swivel chair that used to be his dad's.

He sent her a wary glance. "What's this about?"

"You'll see." She turned on the new computer she'd asked him to buy for her when she started in as top hand.

"What?" he demanded, his senses so full of her, he thought he'd explode.

"Don't be so impatient. Give it a chance to boot up." She leaned over his chair, her gaze on the computer screen, that fragrant hair swinging forward. He watched, transfixed, as she tucked that golden hank of loose hair back behind her ear. He stared at her profile and longed to reach up and run the back of his hand down the smooth golden skin of her throat, to get a fistful of that shining hair and bring it to his mouth so he could feel the silkiness against his lips. "There," she announced. By then, she had her hand on the mouse. She started clicking. "Look at that." She beamed with pride.

He tore his hungry gaze from her face and made himself look at the monitor. "Okay. A spreadsheet."

She laughed. The musical sound seemed to shiver all through him. "Oh, come on. Who's got the fancy business degree from UM? Not me, that's for sure." She pointed. "Look. That's a lot of calves, wouldn't you say? And look at the totals in the yearling column. They're high. I think it's going to be a fine year."

He peered closer at the spreadsheet, frowning. She was right. The yearling count *was* pretty high. He muttered gruffly, "Not bad…"

"I'm working on making sure they're all nice and fat come shipping day. And as far as the calves? I think the total is high there because of that new feed mixture I gave their mamas before calving time. Healthy cows make healthy calves." She laughed again. "Well, duh.

As if you didn't know. And you just watch. Next year, when those calves are ready for market, they'll be weighing in at close to seven hundred pounds each—which is really what I'm leading up to here. Yeah, my new feed mixture is looking like a real success. But bottom line? Winter feeding is expensive. Not only because of all the hay we have to put up, but also in the labor-intensive work of caring for and feeding our pregnant cows in the winter months when the feed has got be brought to them. If you really stop and think about it, *we* work for the cows. My idea is to start letting our cows work for us, letting them find their own feed, which they would do, if there was any available during the winter months…"

He watched her mouth move and kept thinking about what it might feel like under his. What it might *taste* like…

She gave him a big smile. "There are changes going on in the industry, Grant. Ranchers are learning that just because a thing has always been done a certain way doesn't automatically mean it's the best, most efficient and profitable way. What I'm getting to here is that lots of ranchers now are switching from spring to summer calving. And you know what?"

He cleared his throat. "Uh. What?"

"It's working for them, Grant. Matching the nutritional needs of the herd to the forage available can cut production costs and improve profitabil…" Her sweet, husky voice trialed off. "Grant? You with me here?"

"Yeah."

"You seem…distracted."

"No. Really. I'm not."

She leaned in a little closer to him, a tiny frown forming between her smooth brows, the amazing scent of her taunting him even more cruelly that a moment before. "Is it…" She spoke so softly, almost shyly, the savvy ranch foreman suddenly replaced by a nervous young girl. "…about earlier?"

He flat out could not think. His mind was one big ball of mush. "Uh. Earlier?"

A flush swept up her satiny throat and stained her cheeks a tempting pink. "Um. You know. At the creek…" Her gold-tipped lashes swept down. And she swore. A very bad word.

It shocked him enough that he let out a laugh. "Steph. Shame on you."

With a low, frustrated sound, she straightened and stepped back. He felt equal parts relief and despair—relief that she was far enough away he wasn't quite so tempted to grab her. Despair that the delicious smell of her no longer swam all around him.

"Damn it," she said—a much milder oath that time. "I am so…dumb. Just…really, completely childish and dumb."

"Uh. Steph."

*"What?"* She glared at him.

"What are you talking about?"

She flung out a hand. "Oh, please. You know exactly what I'm talking about."

"Er. I do?"

"I keep…beating this silly dead horse to death over and over again. It's just not that huge a deal that you saw me naked, right?" She looked at him pleadingly.

For her sake—and his—he told a whopper of a lie. "No. Not at all. Not a huge deal at all."

"Exactly. It's no big deal and I need to act like a grown-up and let it go. But no. Every time you look at me funny, I'm just sure you're thinking how annoyed or amused or…*whatever* you are at me and it gets me all…flustered and I instantly start babbling away about the whole stupid thing all over again. Oh, I just… Will somebody shoot me? Please. Will somebody just put me clean out of my misery?"

He rose. "Steph."

She put up a hand. "Oh, wait. I know you're going to say something nice. That's how you are. Always so good. So understanding. So…um…" Her eyes widened as he did exactly what he shouldn't do and closed the distance between them. "Wonderful…" she whispered. "Just a wonderful man."

Getting close again was bad enough. But the last thing he ought to do was to put his hands on her. He knew that. He did.

So why the hell was he reaching out and clasping her shoulders?

Damn. Her bones felt so delicate. And the warm silk of her skin where the red shirt ended and her flesh began…

There were no words for that, for the miracle of her skin under his hands. There was nothing.

But the scent of her, the *feel* of her…

She swallowed. "Grant?"

He remembered to speak. "I'm not that wonderful. Take my word for it."

"Oh, Grant…"

"And I want you to know…" The thing was, he could stand here holding her shoulders and looking in her shining eyes for the next decade or so. Just stand here and stare at that dimple in her chin, at her slightly parted lips, her clover-green eyes…

"What?" she asked.

He frowned and, like an idiot, he parroted, "What?"

"You want me to know, what?" Wildly she scanned his face.

And he had no idea what. Not a hint. Not a clue.

And something was happening. Something was changing.

Something about Steph. She was…suddenly different. All at once her nervousness, her girlish embarrassment, had vanished.

Now, he looked down at a woman, a beautiful woman, a woman sure of what she wanted.

"Oh, Grant…" They were the same words she'd said not a minute before.

The same.

And yet totally different.

She lifted her hands and rested them on his chest and before he could remember that he should stop her, she slid them up to encircle his neck.

He shouldn't be doing this, shouldn't be standing here way too close to her, shouldn't be looking down at that mouth of hers, thinking how he'd like nothing better than to cover it with his own.

He shouldn't…

"Oh, Grant. Oh, yeah." And she lifted up on tiptoe and pressed that soft, wide mouth to his.

\* \* \* \*

*Don't forget*
**The Man Who Had Everything**
*is available in July 2008.*

# Two men have vowed to protect the women they love…

New York Times bestselling author

**DIANA PALMER**

*Hard to Handle*

### Hunter

On a top secret operation in the desert, chief of security Hunter knew Jennifer Marist needed his protection. Soon he discovered the lure of Jenny's wild, sweet passion – and a love he'd never dreamed possible.

### Man in Control

Eight years after DEA agent Alexander Cobb had turned Jodie Clayburn down, Alexander could hardly believe the beauty that Jodie had become… or that she'd helped him crack a dangerous drug-smuggling case. Would the man in control finally surrender to his desires?

## Available 20th June 2008

## MILLS & BOON
# *Special* Edition

## On sale 20th June 2008

### The Cowboy's Lullaby
*by Judy Duarte*

When Jake Braddock got joint custody of his little sister, he also got Chloe Haskell in the bargain. With a background as colourful as her red hair, Chloe had little in common with Jake – except her love of the child. Nevertheless, the Texas businessman and the San Francisco dance teacher were soon partners…

### The Reluctant Heiress
*by Christine Flynn*

Discovering she was the secret daughter of a rich senator who had married royalty was no fairy tale for teacher Jillian Hadley. Handsome publicist Ben Garrett came to help protect Jillian from blackmail and malicious gossip. But did the cynical spin doctor himself need a strategy for resisting this vulnerable, alluring woman?

### The Doctor's Secret Child
*by Kate Welsh*

Trey Westerly had arrived on Caroline's doorstep claiming to be the father of her adopted son and it was soon clear that Trey wanted the best for him – even if that meant taking him away from the only home he'd ever known. But Trey's interest was not limited to his son…

## 4 Books
### and a surprise gift!

We would like to take this opportunity to thank you for reading this Mills & Boon® book by offering you the chance to take FOUR more specially selected titles from the Special Edition series absolutely FREE! We're also making this offer to introduce you to the benefits of the Mills & Boon® Reader Service™—

- ★ FREE home delivery
- ★ FREE gifts and competitions
- ★ FREE monthly Newsletter
- ★ Exclusive Reader Service offers
- ★ Books available before they're in the shops

Accepting these FREE books and gift places you under no obligation to buy, you may cancel at any time, even after receiving your free shipment. Simply complete your details below and return the entire page to the address below. You don't even need a stamp!

**YES!** Please send me 4 free Special Edition books and a surprise gift. I understand that unless you hear from me, I will receive 6 superb new titles every month for just £3.15 each, postage and packing free. I am under no obligation to purchase any books and may cancel my subscription at any time. The free books and gift will be mine to keep in any case.

E8ZEF

Ms/Mrs/Miss/Mr ....................................................Initials.......................

**BLOCK CAPITALS PLEASE**

Surname ......................................................................................................

Address...........................................................................................................

...........................................................................................................

.......................................................................Postcode ..........................

### Send this whole page to:
### UK: FREEPOST CN81, Croydon, CR9 3WZ